THE
QUANTUM THEORY
OF **LOVE**
AND **MADNESS**

Essential Prose Series 176

Canada Council
for the Arts

Conseil des Arts
du Canada

ONTARIO ARTS COUNCIL
CONSEIL DES ARTS DE L'ONTARIO

an Ontario government agency
un organisme du gouvernement de l'Ontario

Canadä

Guernica Editions Inc. acknowledges the support of the Canada Council
for the Arts and the Ontario Arts Council. The Ontario Arts Council
is an agency of the Government of Ontario.

We acknowledge the financial support of the Government of Canada.

THE QUANTUM THEORY OF LOVE  AND MADNESS

stories

Jerry Levy

GUERNICA
EDITIONS
TORONTO • BUFFALO • LANCASTER (U.K.)
2020

Michael Mirolla, editor
David Moratto, cover and Interior design
Guernica Editions Inc.
287 Templemead Drive, Hamilton (ON), Canada L8W 2W4
2250 Military Road, Tonawanda, N.Y. 14150-6000 U.S.A.
www.guernicaeditions.com

Distributors:
Independent Publishers Group (IPG)
600 North Pulaski Road, Chicago IL 60624
University of Toronto Press Distribution,
5201 Dufferin Street, Toronto (ON), Canada M3H 5T8
Gazelle Book Services, White Cross Mills
High Town, Lancaster LA1 4XS U.K.

First edition.
Printed in Canada.

Legal Deposit—First Quarter
Library of Congress Catalog Card Number: 2019946495
Library and Archives Canada Cataloguing in Publication
Title: The quantum theory of love and madness : stories / Jerry Levy.
Names: Levy, Jerry, author.
Series: Essential prose series ; 176.
Description: First edition. | Series statement: Essential prose series ; 176
Identifiers: Canadiana (print) 20190153083 | Canadiana (ebook)
2019015313X | ISBN 9781771834766 (softcover) |
ISBN 9781771834773 (EPUB) | ISBN 9781771834780 (Kindle)
Classification: LCC PS8623.E959 Q36 2020 | DDC C813/.6—dc23

Contents

THE ARSONIST

ONCE, **THERE WAS** a place I could go where no one would bother me, where I could feel safe. The heavy burden that seemed to perpetually weigh me down was lifted, and I could breathe easily, fluidly. It was so quiet there, just me and books. Of course, there were other people at the library but they just went about their business and never bothered anyone—perhaps they too felt the way I did.

I was 17 when I first felt the need to go there, to my refuge. I had been taking care of Evan, my 12-year-old brother, for about a year. Ever since our parents were killed in an automobile accident. It was a head-on crash on a country road and the police told me they died instantly; apparently my father, who was driving, had veered over the centre line ever so slightly. But that's all it took on this narrow road.

I was hardly capable of taking care of Evan ... I was just a kid myself. But when the Social Services lady came around, I lied and told her I was already working part-time as a waitress, making decent money. I also let them know that our aunt Edna would be coming over daily. That would have been dandy had there been an Aunt Edna. In fact, we had no relatives to speak of. None we could rely on anyway. It was true that we did have an aunt—Aunt Julia, my mother's sister. But she and mom had long ago had a falling out and, when my parents died, she was nowhere to be seen. Grudges don't die very fast, it seems. And as for my father, he was an orphan. No family that anyone knew.

We had enough money, that much was certain—our dad was a tax accountant and made sure my brother and I were well taken of. The will said that, with the exception of $20,000 which was earmarked for the SPCA, all the money was to go to the kids. I didn't mind, I had a soft spot for animals as well. And besides, Evan and I now had something like $850,000 in the bank. Given that the mortgage was already paid off, and a trust fund set up, we could've retired. Ha, imagine—two young kids, our whole lives in front of us, and the path to Oz, full of fun and adventure, lay beckoning.

So I didn't have to lie about being a waitress to the nice lady from Social Services, but I just wanted her to think I was a responsible human being. Funny thing was, after I spouted out all that nonsense about working and Aunt Edna, the woman left our house, quite satisfied … she didn't seem to check anything out. She only arranged for a social worker to come in once a week, and for Evan and me to continue attending school. And she made me promise to give up the waitressing, saying I had enough on my plate with school and taking care of my brother. That was it.

And so there we were, my brother and I, lounging about in this big house. Evan went to the window and stuck his tongue out at the Social Services lady as she drove away and I hurriedly took off my crisp white blouse, plaid skirt and polished black shoes—the uniform that helped me pretend to be an adult—and got into my torn jeans, sandals, and Justin Bieber t-shirt. I made dinner for Evan—a big bowl of buttered popcorn—and settled down to watch a movie. Something about teens on Spring break down in Ft. Lauderdale. Lots of booze, lots of sex, lots of carousing. No responsibilities. It spoke to me, that movie did. I could've starred in it, why not. I was a teen, I had the money, and boy, was I ready for sex. But really, I couldn't, not with a young brother to bring up. So I just went to bed that night and pleasured myself, and oh my God, did it ever feel good. Since Evan had crashed out on the sofa in the living room while watching TV, I continued my lovely sexual exploits all night long.

In case you're wondering, we did cry. Both Evan and me. For many weeks. Months even. It was hard to believe that our parents were dead and that we were alone. Sometimes Evan would sit at the window and look out, as if he half-expected them to come home. Evan blamed them though, saying they were reckless and had no right to die while we were so young ... we needed them. We did, but I repeatedly explained to him that shit happens, things people have no control over, and that you couldn't blame Mom and Dad—we were just lucky we weren't in the car with them. That seemed to mollify Evan, and he shook his head in agreement. Still, I always wondered whether he really ever got over the loss.

I think the worst part—if there could ever be anything worse than losing one's parents—is that I felt so alone. An invisible person. And somehow quite unsafe. I knew there was nothing really to fear, because we were set up for life. But I felt unsure of myself and my ability to be a caregiver. The truth was that I could hardly care for myself. I tried though, I really did. Every day I made peanut butter and jam sandwiches for Evan and me to take to school. Sometimes bologna and cheese. Salami and mustard. I threw in an apple or a Pop Tart and a can of orange juice. It worked I guess, whatever 'worked' meant, but it didn't feel right. Not nurturing enough, not healthy enough, not good enough. I just didn't have it in me to do any better. The social worker saw both of us growing and figured everything was alright, that Aunt Edna knew her way around a kitchen. I even adopted the moniker "Aunt Edna' when cooking, which never failed to elicit gales of laughter from Evan.

Still, I did learn to do things, even if they never felt quite accomplished enough. I learned to do the laundry and became mesmerized by the dryer, watching the clothes tumble round and round, like I was watching some crazed merry-go-round. An inverted one. I can't say it was better than watching music videos on my phone but sometimes, it was pretty darn close.

Despite the occasional bouts of laughter, Evan, like me, was often scared. Seemingly, he was chased by invisible ghosts. He refused to sleep in his bed, saying that monsters were waiting underneath; according to him, as soon as the lights were closed, they would emerge to kill him.

"So keep your nightlight on," I said.

"I'm still scared," he said.

So we slept in our parents' bed together every night for years. The big sprawling bed with the king-sized duvet covered with red roses and the fluffy oversized pillows. It was warm there, and comforting, like sleeping under a huge pile of flowers, so I didn't mind at all. Before nodding off, we would say goodnight to our parents, kissing the framed picture of them that was on the nightstand.

But it soon became obvious to us that we needed company. If truth be known, we had plenty—the neighbours. As soon as they found out about our parents, they came over on a regular basis. Mrs. Wilson brought us homemade food—lasagna, apple and cherry pies, cabbage rolls (which caused Evan to mockingly stick his finger down his throat), stews, chicken, hamburgers, meatloaf with mashed potatoes and gravy. So much food you would have thought we would explode sometimes, which is probably the real reason we continued growing. Many other neighbours dropped by to check on us, and to keep us company. Mr. Shuster would come over every Saturday morning, make himself a cup of tea, and sit at the kitchen table, reading the newspaper. We couldn't talk to him, he was so engrossed. He didn't seem to want to converse anyway. It was just as well; he seemed like an old dude to us, maybe like over 40 or so. After about two hours, he would take off his reading glasses, fold up the paper, and say: "Well, that's it, kids. Good meeting with you. See you next week." And Mrs. Perlwinkler bought Evan and me big green rubber galoshes and cloth gardening gloves, so we could keep up the garden our parents tended in the front yard. She helped of course. It was fun getting dirty but really, we didn't know anything about plants. Nor did we care. Still, the company was good, and we found a lot of worms.

But my brother and I longed for a different kind of

company. The animal kind. We briefly considered a dog but realized it would take too much work. We settled on a cat. So one Saturday morning, we bicycled to the SPCA and tried to adopt one. *Too young*, they said. Then we reminded them that our dad donated $20,000 to their organization.

We named the tabby cat 'CookieBear.' Just a cozy, light name. A warm name. She was maybe three months old and rambunctious as hell, making mad dashes throughout the house, knocking things over, climbing the curtains. Talk about being chased by invisible ghosts, CookieBear was inhabited by a poltergeist, I was pretty certain. But getting her was the best thing we could have done. Suddenly, the big house was spilling over with life once more. She was nothing less than a crazy ball of frenetic energy, and most importantly, she was unafraid of anything. She also demanded that we make a place for her every night on the big bed we slept in. So then it became the three of us—me, Evan, and CookieBear, the latter licking our faces with her rough tongue and purring away like a soft outboard motor, until she fell asleep. And it was then, just before I myself was about to nod off, that I felt invincible. Like nothing ever again could hurt me.

Oh, I certainly tried to make a home for Evan. In many ways, we had one ... a somewhat contented one. Sort of. We had our routines—five mornings a week I would walk him to school, my hand in his, and every afternoon pick him up. We had regular meals, and I learned to make things he really liked, like grilled cheese sandwiches (with two cheeses, Gouda and Swiss) and potato chips, even spaghetti with warmed-over frozen meatballs. And we had all of Mrs. Wilson's food. We also splurged once or twice a week on pepperoni and pineapple pizza, or chicken and fries from Swiss Cluck. We went to bed on time. Mostly we did. Like no later than midnight on weeknights. Only a bit later on weekends. We hired a maid to come in once a week and clean up. It was like a regular family, except without the parents. And we both went to school, and made friends. Well, not *really* friends. More like acquaintances. I think we felt that the other kids lived a totally different experience than us. And of course they did. But even that was ok, acquaintances were good too.

Despite all that, despite my very best efforts, my brother was suffering. I would sometimes find him crouched in a corner of his room, crying. When I'd ask what the matter was, he would simply shrug. He didn't know, or maybe he did but wouldn't tell me. But he didn't have to say a word, because I knew. Because I often felt the same way.

I worried about him. It wasn't only the crying spells. There was something else. Once our neighbours Mr. and Mrs. Dawkins took us to an Amish village, where we drank warm milk straight from a cow, tasted sweet raspberry and blueberry jams, ate delicious peanut brittle, rode in a horse and buggy, and toured an old wooden school and a red barn that was filled with chickens. It was a full day. At one point, I noticed that Evan had wandered off and was standing next to a barb-wired fence. I hurried to catch up.

"Look at this," he said. Stuck in a barb was a white t-shirt and Evan pulled a match from his pocket and set it alight.

"Stop!" I shouted, pulling his arm away.

But it was too late. The t-shirt blazed away, smoke filled the air, and people came running.

I lied to everyone and said that Evan and I came sprinting over when we saw the flames. No one thought anything of it, and soon the matter was forgotten. Not by me though, and I snuck angry glances at him throughout the car ride back to the city. I could've wrung his neck; he was going to spoil it all for us, our little contented family. Because it wasn't the first time he set fire to something. Two weeks prior to the Amish trip, he had gathered a pile of twigs together in our backyard and struck a match. I saw him do it. I took a garden hose and doused the flames.

"Are you crazy?" I said. "That small fire could've burnt down all the trees back here. Started a real forest fire. Shit!" I snatched the matches from him and stuck them in my pocket.

It was then, after those two episodes, that I found my safe haven in the local library. I had always been drawn to books, first the Nancy Drew detective series, and later on more serious literature. Unlike my real life, I felt totally safe within the world of fiction. The circumstances of my life didn't allow me to travel, that was obvious, but within the pages of the many novels I read, I traveled the world. And the assorted characters that filled my head taught me much about how to live; they were the best teachers I could have had.

I always picked the same seat at the library; it was tucked away in a corner, near the washroom, and usually empty. I suspected no one wanted to sit there because there was a big wall clock right above, and you could literally hear the seconds tick away. It was annoying for sure but I got used to it and became grateful for it. And certainly, I was grateful for the library itself—as soon as I set foot within, I was able to relax and the heavy burden that seemed to continually stress me, began to dissipate.

I loved reading fiction so much that I decided to major in English Literature in university. It just seemed natural; I didn't have to worry much about getting a job that paid big bucks and books made me happy. So why not? With that in mind, after my undergraduate degree, I went on to enrol in a Publishing programme and I found the very thing I wanted to do with my life. Like many of the people I encountered in university, I tried my hand at writing poetry and prose. But I quickly realized I wasn't much good at it and that I was much more suited for the business side of the book world, championing authors. It was all too easy, and once I got a job at a small independent publisher, not one day felt like 'work.' The money wasn't great but I met many authors and editors, and hung around like-minded people. And maybe the best thing is that the fear I felt after my parents died slowly started disappearing. I even made some real friends.

If only Evan had developed that same love of literature. If only. I tried to get him reading by buying Archie and Richie Rich comics, then Hardy Boy books. But he thought it was all a waste of time, getting immersed in a world that wasn't real. He preferred pictures to the words. I patiently explained to him the eccentric and outlandish characters in Charles Dickens, like Old Bill Barley in *Great Expectations*, Fagin in *Oliver Twist*, Uriah Heep in *David Copperfield* ... the list was quite endless. And I told him that Dickens himself didn't have an easy childhood, having left school at an early age to work in a blacking factory when his father was incarcerated in a debtors' prison. That piqued Evan's interest, but only temporarily. A few years after our parents' deaths, and some time after the two fire-related episodes, he started to hang around with a rough crowd. Like me, he couldn't easily make friends but with his group of ruffians, he found kindred spirits, broken, disillusioned youths. He told me they all had their own tales of woe, not unlike himself. So he started drinking, smoking dope, often staying away from home for days. Despite my protestations, he dropped out of school.

One day, after a binge drinking marathon that Evan advised had gone on for three days, he came home with a tattoo on his left forearm. We were Jewish by birth and we both knew that it was strictly forbidden in Judaism to tattoo oneself—I learned as much from Mom and Dad, and I passed that on to Evan.

"I was drunk," he protested.

I held his arm in my hand and scrutinized the strange markings. There was a full moon and twinkling stars in a night sky, the moon moving behind some clouds and turning into a crescent. Above the scene were the cryptic words: "FADING AWAY."

"What's all this crap?" I said.

"The moon was full at some point, as you can see," he explained. "But over time, it starts to vanish. Clever, huh?"

"No." I threw his arm down in disgust and walked away.

Maybe the thing that caused Evan's precipitous descent is when we lost CookieBear. Sure my brother was already showing signs of being a brat by wandering off occasionally with some bad guys, but with our cat gone, he seemed to lose all hope. "Nothing ever lasts," he told me.

We used to let the cat out to roam about. We always knew where she was, just lollygagging about the neighbourhood, sitting on porches, sleeping on front lawns, cozying up to people for a scratch behind the neck. She always came home every night to eat, play, and sleep with us. But one day she didn't come home. We searched for her all over, even put up posters, but nothing. And that was that.

I was failing my brother, my flesh and blood, but I didn't know what to do. I had tried my best but it was obvious my best wasn't good enough. I never had the skills, never the wisdom. All the prayers I said, not to some nebulous God, but rather to Mom and Dad, asking for guidance, seemed to have gone unheeded.

We continued living in the same big house but over time, it seemed different, lonely, just like it had been immediately after our parents died. With CookieBear gone, my time at school, and Evan staying away for extended periods of time, all life there was gone and when I was home, I walked the rooms like a dispirited ghost. And when we were together, Evan and I, we seemed to have nothing to say to each other.

One day, I heard about a fire at a local flower shop. I knew the place, Mrs. Perlwinkler had taken us there on a number of occasions over the years. The police said the fire had been deliberately set. I thought nothing of it, until a rash of such fires broke out in the neighbourhood—at a deli, a restaurant, a pop-up clothing shop. A spate of bad luck? It seemed not, the police were now quite sure they were dealing with a serial arsonist. I had no reason to suspect Evan, until a TV news broadcast showed the interior of the charred restaurant where it appeared, to my disbelieving eyes, that a crescent moon crudely drawn on a standing wall lay hidden behind some clouds.

"Fuck you," I spat at my brother when he one day walked through the front door of our house. "I'm going to turn you in."

"Like hell you are."

He nonchalantly walked into the kitchen, took a quart of chocolate milk, and retired to his own bedroom.

He was right—I couldn't turn him in, not after all we had been through. It was unthinkable. But I wondered why he risked drawing attention to himself with the illustration on the wall; someone other than me might have recognized it. Did he perhaps want to be caught?

A few days later I got my answer. And it struck me then that Evan would certainly have known how his actions would affect me, since he had long been aware of my first love. He had also been right—nothing ever does last. There are also no goodbyes, people and animals just fall off the ends of the earth when you least expect it and are gone from your life. All those thoughts came to me as I stood with tears in my eyes and watched, alongside a large group of people, as flames engulfed my beloved library. It was then, my hands shaking, that I found myself using my cell phone to call the police.

PARIS WAS THE RAGE

THE WOMAN SITTING opposite on the subway was reading a book—*Tangential Relationships of Parallel and Alternate Universes*. The title unnerved me. Not only was I not exactly certain what 'tangential' meant but I had never spent any time contemplating parallel universes, whatever they were. In the pedestrian world of the underground transit system —where the Harlequins and Barbara Cartlands ruled— the book seemed distinctly uncommon.

Beset with curiosity, I sidled into the empty seat next to her and surreptitiously glanced at the book. What I saw were two circles that appeared to very slightly intersect in the middle, much like the kind of stuff I once disdained in Grade 9 Geometry.

The woman smiled. "Interested in parallel universes?"

"No, not especially," I stammered. "It was just the circles that caught my attention."

"It's about parallel worlds but also time travel," the woman prattled on, ignoring what I had just said. "Even alternate realities. So many things off the beaten track, ones we rarely think about. Like how your life might have been vastly different, maybe happier, if only you had made another choice. Taken another path. So interesting."

"Like I said, it was just the circles that caught my eye. I'm not too interested in 'what if's,' I'm afraid. I'm firmly rooted in the *here and now*."

It wasn't exactly true—the whole notion of another universe that paralleled the one I was living in seemed abundantly fascinating. Yet I couldn't admit as much. Embarrassed by my answer, I exited at the next subway station and waited for another train car in order to resume my journey. I mulled over the word 'tangential'—something I vaguely recalled having touched on in some high school class, maybe that same Geometry one—and surmised that it meant 'close to,' or 'touching.' Something like that anyway.

That night, as had been my habit of late, I woke at the most ungodly hour of 3 am and made my way to the washroom. Weak bladder. This time though, I was infused with a sense of dread. Why that should have been I did not know. I mean, my life was pretty good. I had a stable, decent-paying job as an insurance underwriter and was married to a caring woman with whom I had two terrific kids. Just to ensure that all was copasetic, I peeked into my son's room. Then my daughter's. They were both fast asleep.

I returned to the washroom and breathed deeply as urine splashed into the toilet bowl.

Once again, I was filled with that same sense of dread.

When I was a kid, I liked to play at murder mysteries. As the last drops of urine fell languidly, I suddenly had visions of standing before my battalion of childhood friends, playing 'whodunit.' I saw myself with a Sherlock Holmes cap on and a tartan cape wrapped around my small shoulders, trying to decipher a murder. There were many suspects to choose from and a multitude of clues from which to draw a conclusion. Everyone had fake blood on their hands, everyone wore a sneer that suggested they were infinitely smarter than me and would get away with the crime. But it didn't matter; as Holmes, I always got my man.

Why those childhood images suddenly bubbled into my mind I could not say. But, while they perhaps should have assuaged my anxiety—since in fact it was a joyful time, they didn't. They did the exact opposite in fact and made me more agitated. I returned to bed and lay next to my wife but did not sleep for the rest of the night.

In the morning, I made coffee and toast. My daughter Emma diverted my attention and so the toast burnt ... but I ate it anyway. I drove from my suburban house to the subway station and hopped on the 6:55 am train, the same one I took every day. As usual, it was standing room only. I looked around—many people were sleeping, others reading newspapers, and still others bopping their heads and silently mouthing words that emanated from headphones. The train screeched, stopping for inordinately long periods of time at certain stations, sometimes between stations, and then continued on.

Debarking at my final destination, I joined the long queue at Timmie's along with other office workers and some construction workers, and then bought two muffins—banana-walnut and apple cinnamon, and a large cup of java, double-double. Along with the bag of jelly-beans I always kept at my desk, the sugary muffins kept me going all day long.

At the office, I walked absently to the kitchen and buttered my muffins, using someone else's butter. I did it nearly every day, stealing from the fridge. Everyone did it. Food was always going missing and the office manager would dutifully send out e-mails reminding everyone of the dire consequences of pilferage ... 20 lashes or some such thing. I never read the e-mails and relegated them to the Trash bin as soon as they arrived. I took a large bite of the banana-walnut muffin and then quickly returned the butter to the exact spot in the fridge where I had taken it, trying to somehow wrap it so that no one would notice that the bar was getting progressively smaller.

Late that very night, something came over me, a mania of sorts, and as I exited from my usual late-night foray into the washroom, I headed straight to the basement. Like a person possessed, as if I were trying to quell an unknown fear, I searched through boxes containing my old university texts. Interestingly, while I always found the sciences and maths especially difficult throughout school, I had a certain affinity for the more aesthetic courses—subjects like history and literature.

I found one book—*English Romantic Poets of the 18th Century*. I flipped through the pages and came across a poem by William Blake entitled 'London,' one in which I had scribbled tiny notes in the margins. I tried to read what I had written many years earlier but couldn't—it was simply undecipherable. Chicken scratch. But then a strange thing happened. The more I read through the poem, the more I started remembering. *This is Blake's protest poem to social conditions,* I thought. I had once recited the entire poem by rote. Now, as I read about "the youthful harlot's curse," and "the mind-forged manacles," I was overtaken with waves of sheer joy. I couldn't explain it but reading the poem was exhilarating. I also started to recognize some of my scribbling: 'Blake *marks* and *hears* human suffering ...' I could not make out the rest. I held the book tightly to my chest a long time.

In the morning, I asked my wife whether she knew that Blake had been a visionary, seen angels in trees.

"I don't know what you're saying," she said tersely. "Are you talking Robert Blake? The actor who played in that detective show *Baretta* back in I think the seventies? The one who always kept a cockatoo on his shoulder?"

"No, not him."

"They say he shot his wife. But it was never proved."

"Huh." I slathered peanut butter onto my toast and took a hard bite.

"She had many enemies, so you never know," she said. "The only other 'Blake' I know is Blake Lively. She was in *The Sisterhood of the Traveling Pants*."

So I explained, all the while my wife staring at me as if I were some virus from another planet. I couldn't blame her. Why would she know William Blake, the 18th century poet and painter? My wife was into 21st century actors, could talk endlessly about who had starred in which movies, who was dating whom, which sitcoms were awesome. When I married her, I knew what I was getting. A college dropout, a little frumpy, definitely not a wordsmith or intellectual, but like I said, a caregiver ... that was most important.

"So why are you telling me this?" she blurted suddenly.

"Well ... "

"Some obscure poet that nobody ever heard of? Really. What's come over you lately? Instead of daydreaming, I've got a better idea—can you help get the kids ready for school please. That would be useful."

I hurriedly ate the last of my toast. The kids, yes, of course. It was always about them. I wasn't complaining. Just part of the deal of being a dad. I loved it ... the little ones, the running around. Hockey practice, ballet. Helping with homework. Seeing them grow. Ok, there was no mental stimulation but so what? I could always get what I needed that way from my colleagues at work.

When I got there, the place that paid my wages, I had a little free time and decided, quite on the spur of the moment, to look up my old university girlfriend. Another strange mania ... maybe I really was becoming possessed. After all, close to twenty-five years had passed since I had last seen Claire Martin. I can't say I had never thought of her all those years. But not for long. Why would I? My life was full. And, with the exception of my late-night bathroom visits where I recalled my childhood escapades as Sherlock, I was never one to particularly dwell on the past. Of course, I understood it was all that rummaging through my old university texts that had provided the nudge. No doubt, because it was in English class where Claire and I had met. The very one where we had studied not only Blake, but Byron, Shelly, and Keats. The attractive woman I always thought I might marry. Too bad she didn't have the same idea.

So why did I feel compelled to look her up all these years later? Sure she had been the prettiest woman I ever dated. And undoubtedly the smartest. What was not to like?

She wasn't hard to track down. A few phone calls to her old law firm. And a Google and Facebook search of 'Claire Martin.' Buoyed, I called her home phone number. Then I hung up after the second ring.

Who was I kidding? Mental stimulation from work colleagues? The place was a wasteland. T.S. Eliot's *The Waste Land*. No one read, no one went to films other than Hollywood blockbusters, no one talked of ideas. It was all about family life, houses in the 'burbs, holiday vacation at all-inclusive Caribbean resorts. They were all good people and I got along splendidly ... as long as I didn't veer off the required trajectory. And in some respects, because I had for so long now talked the way they did, acted the way they did, I had lost good chunks of myself anyway. Chunks of the past. I now knew a lot more about the Kardashians than I did about Browning, Keats, Dickens, and the other scribes I had once so revered.

I had to try again. So I closed the door to my office and redialled. I saw myself going through the motions, like I was looking in on myself from the outside. A stranger punching in Claire Martin's phone number. My hands were shaking and my throat had dried up. I loosened my tie.

"Hello?" A child's sing-song voice.

"Hi there."

"Who is it?"

"It's a friend of your mother's. Can I talk to her please?"

"Ma! Somebody on the phone for you!"

"Tell them I'm busy and I'll call back! Ask who it is please, Jennifer!" Ah, that melodic voice, a distant memory. Interspersed into the ether.

"I think she's maybe in the bathroom. She wants to know who it is."

"Just tell her it's an old friend."

"Ma, he says he doesn't know!"

I hung up. Then I opened the door to my office and looked out—my next client was waiting. I wiped the sweat from my forehead, took a few deep breaths, and quietly closed the door. *There was always the next client, the next meeting.*

I sat in my car outside Claire Martin's grand home. It was in the east end of the city, an upscale two-storey detached that had clearly been renovated. I didn't know this area very well, only that it had become gentrified ... and the homes were getting astronomically pricey. I suppose I could have hired a private investigator to do the job. He'd sit in a car and sip on cold coffee, pretending to be otherwise engaged. But I wasn't even sure what I wanted from the woman. Even if she were single, no boyfriend.

Images of my wife suddenly bubbled into my mind and I exhaled deeply. We were still at odds over our upcoming vacation. I asked her to consider Paris, someplace we had never been. The *City of Lights*. Home to all the writers and artists that once forged so much of my imagination—

Hemingway, Gertrude and Alice, Picasso, Sartre, Manet, Degas, Beckett, Rimbaud, Baudelaire. So many, so many. Paris was the rage, there was no doubt. I wanted to walk in my heroes' footsteps, drink *une absinthe* in Les Deux Magots. Maybe read a book there. Linger and watch people go by as I fondled *un café espresso* in Café de Flore. Venture to Shakespeare & Company, the English-language bookstore started by Sylvia Beach in the 1920's. The very one that served as a meeting place for many American and English expatriates living in Paris at the time. I wanted to gaze out at the Seine, to see if I could spot her curve as she divides around the Île de la Cité and the Île Saint-Louis. A woman's face is what it purportedly looks like, her eyes closed, up-turned for a kiss. I had read that Paris' bus and Metro administration used this image as its trademark. And why not? Paris had always been the city of romance.

I tried to impress these things upon my wife but she only gave me a nasty look, like I was trying her patience. I knew that look; I had seen it many times before, especially at the very beginning of our relationship when I talked books with her. Or tried to. But that look, it was unmistak-able. It now said: *What, tell me, is wrong with the Dominican Republic? Five-Star resorts, frolicking in the ocean, all-you-can-eat buffets? Now that's a **real** vacation.*

"You can drink an espresso at home," she said in words that accompanied the look. "Didn't I get you one of those machines at Christmas. You never even use it. And if you're so interested, I can even buy you rot-gut absinthe for the occasional drink. Anyway, think the kids want to go schlepping through boring art galleries in some old Euro-pean city? Or looking at stained glass in a church?" There was no question, my wife was in step with my work colleagues. One mind.

I looked at my watch. It was just after 7:30 in the morning and all the lights in Claire's house were turned on. I figured the early morning was the best time to catch her; most everyone left their homes then. And I was right. At a few minutes before 8 am, I slithered low into the driver's seat as she and her brood exited. Well, I recognized that face at once. I could never forget it. Older of course but still exceptionally pretty, she took my breath away.

I remained hidden until the car sped away. Then I came up for air and ran my hands through my hair. I looked at my watch. I was running late for work and called the office to let them know. Then I spilled out the rest of my putrid coffee through the open driver's window.

When I walked into the office, I saw that a client was already sitting there, waiting for me. Christ, I had forgotten the appointment! I shook hands, apologized for my tardiness, asked if he wanted a coffee (he did) and told him to wait right there. I hurried to the lunchroom and filled a cup.

My client rose from his chair when I returned and took the coffee cup. "Thank you, that's great." We talked money and strategy for quite some time, shook hands, and then he departed. Another hand, one of hundreds I had shaken over the years. Limp handshakes, firm handshakes, two-handed ones ... in the end, they were all the same.

I stayed in my office and contemplated my morning thus far, I couldn't believe that I had waited like a teenager in front of my old girlfriend's house. What was happening to me? The office open, I listened to the far murmur of the goings-on in my workplace. Nothing succinct came my way; muffled words wafted to my ears and flew out again, like crazed butterflies. It was like that, if I listened carefully ... a cacophony of muted sounds, nothing really made any sense.

For the next two days, I waited in front of Claire's house and watched her leave. I had no plan, only some vague idea that I might 'accidentally' run into her. Like maybe honk as I pulled up alongside in traffic.

"Oh my God!" she'd sputter as she rolled the window down. "I don't believe it."

Neither did I, for it never happened. Nothing happened, in fact, except I was late to work for another two days.

Three nights later, as 3 am called out to me, I remained in the washroom and wrote on a pad:

> *Declared dead at 3 in the morning*
> *In desperation*
> *I bury you,*
> *the Now.*
> *By the seaside*
> *A flock of gulls*
> *Catch a*
> *Whiff of abandon*
> *In the current*

It wasn't great poetry, I knew. But it didn't matter. I was just glad to get something out—it was like a small miracle after all these years.

I sat on the toilet seat and reread what I had written. Then I thought about the woman in the subway and wondered whether on a parallel universe—if there really were such a thing—I might actually be a half-decent poet, and Claire and I might be an item again. Perhaps I might even have the nerve to tell my wife that I didn't want to drink absinthe in my house; that in fact, I was going to Paris ... alone.

THE WRITER

HE HADN'T WRITTEN but four lines all day and the fine mist of discontent that was slowly settling over him now changed to something more insidious, rankling. *Writers Block* they called it but he knew it was something else, something that went to his very core.

He slowly moved away from his computer and paced the living room. With his mother away, he felt lonely and yet, there was a part of him that wished she would stay away for good. He couldn't forget though that it was her house and he was there solely by the goodness of her heart. Thirty-three years old and he had no way to support himself, nowhere else to go.

He had these illnesses—ADD and depression and something else, something undiagnosed, that caused him to occasionally walk along the border toward alter-realities, to 'live in a dream world,' his mother had sometimes said—and couldn't hold down any job for very long. But he could write, or so he believed, although no publisher would bite on his novels. "Lacking imagination," he was told, ironic given what his mother mentioned.

He would go for a drive; that would settle him down. The white boat he backed out of the driveway, an Eldorado, his mother's car, was a fine showpiece and he enjoyed being seen in it. It made him feel successful.

The bright lights of the big city attracted. For someone who lived in the suburbs, it was always exciting venturing downtown. As he drove closer to the downtown core, he felt more enervated than he had in some time. Positively giddy, as if he could reach up and touch the moon.

"Double double," he barked into the intercom at a drive-in coffee shop. "And a toasted tea biscuit with butter. Make that two."

Ever since his mother had left for an extended vacation to the Greek Islands and through Europe, he found he couldn't eat properly, couldn't prepare his own meals, subsisting on half a dozen tea biscuits and two cans of Ensure each day.

Suddenly there was a hard knock on his passenger window. A wisp of a woman, drenched with rain, stood imploringly.

"I don't have any extra change," he said.

"I didn't ask for change," she replied. "Can you buy me a coffee?"

He considered rolling down the window but thought the better of it.

"It's cold. Please, mister. You look like a nice guy. Like someone I would like to know. Please."

He reluctantly opened the door and let the woman in. "Thanks."

This was no woman. She was a mere girl, fifteen, maybe sixteen.

"What do you take in your coffee?" he asked.

"Anything, thanks," she said nonchalantly, exhaling deeply.

Anything? he wondered. What kind of answer was that? He ordered her a large coffee, one cream, two sugars. And a ham and cheese sandwich.

She cradled her knees up to her chest. There were holes in her running shoes, her jeans were ripped at the knees, and she was shivering. He put the heat on high and watched her wolf down the food. There was a pink, raised-skin brand on her arm that caught his attention.

"Good, huh?"

"Mmm ... "

"My name's Doug Swan," he said.

"That's a funny name ... Swan."

"And you?"

"Sarah."

"That's it? Just *Sarah*?"

"Yah, that's it. Just Sarah. I don't seem to have a last name, none that I can recall anyway."

"OK, Sarah. I'll play along. But you've eaten. So now you'll have to get out."

"Can we just maybe drive around for awhile?" she asked. "I've been waiting a long time."

"Waiting?"

"For a home, you know."

Swan thought about the request. *Waiting for a home?* That was a weird way to phrase things.

"So where can I take you, Sarah?" he said at last. "Maybe to your parents?"

"No parents," she said. "Both dead. I'm on my own. Like I said, no home."

Swan took the least scenic route he knew, meandering through gritty backstreets of the downtown area. The last thing he wanted was to give Sarah the impression that the ride was going to continue for very long.

"Once I rode in a car like this," she said, sipping on her coffee, "and my boyfriend kicked me out the door."

Swan wasn't sure what to make of that. People only got kicked out of moving cars in the movies. Curiously, long ago he had written a short story where a young woman was thrown from a moving car. The story, now vague in his memory, had never gone anywhere and he had abandoned it.

"He was upset because I wouldn't do what he wanted me to do," she said.

"What was that?"

"Sell my body and give him the money. I mean, I did it for a bit but not for long."

Swan turned to look at the stranger that was riding with him. Had he in fact given a ride to a hooker?

The Eldorado continued past the decrepit waterfront, past abandoned warehouses and rows of dilapidated houses in the east end.

"Well, I hope you weren't hurt when you got kicked out. It sounds like it could have been very painful, getting kicked out of a car. I hope it wasn't moving."

"Oh, it was moving alright. But I'm used to pain."

"I'm a writer," Swan said, eager to change the topic. "I wrote poetry once."

"I don't write poetry. Just prose. You know, fiction."

"I know. But why not poetry?"

"Don't like it. I think people who write poetry can't write prose. Inferior talent, if you ask me."

Sarah put her feet down and sagged back into her seat. "I don't think you know what you're talking about, Mr. Swan."

Swan ignored the last remark. He really didn't want to get into a debate about the merits of the written word with a street urchin.

"Are you warm enough now? I can turn the heat down if you are."

Sarah pulled out a soggy pack of cigarettes from her shirt pocket. "Mind if I smoke?" she said, drawing one out before Swan could answer.

As the smoke lazily drifted near his face, Swan thought he'd better get the interior of the car cleaned before his mother returned. Deodorize it or something. But as inconvenient as that was, he in fact didn't mind Sarah smoking—he was starting to realize that having her in the car was better than being alone.

"Aside from writing poetry, what else are you good at?" he asked.

Sarah exhaled a puff of smoke. "I didn't say I was any good at writing poetry, Mr. Swan."

"You've got me there."

"But I know you just want to make conversation," she said. "So I'll tell you I was pretty good in French. Completely self-taught too."

"Really? I don't know French at all. Never learned. Say something."

"Vous êtes un très gentil homme."

"Wow, that's great. I wish I spoke French."

"Wanna know what I said?"

"Sure."

"I said I'd like to see where you live."

Swan looked at Sarah and smiled. *What was she up to? Was it her usual style to get into cars with strange men and ask to go to their homes?*

"What did you have in mind?" Swan asked, uncertain what exactly he was asking.

"Just some talk, Mr. Swan. It'd be nice to talk inside a real house. Mostly I do my talking inside shelters, which, although technically a house, aren't real houses. Know what I mean?"

No problem, thought Swan sarcastically. *With Just Sarah.* He had seen enough movies and TV shoes to know what 'just talk' meant. That was how it always began. The idea started to take hold and appealed to him. Maybe a night of adventure was what he needed. Already his mood was much better than when he had started out the night on his computer. Besides, he had never been with a woman.

The big engine rolled on with renewed vigour, taking the expectant couple through the wilds of the upper-class suburban enclave of Toronto where Swan lived. Row after row of Spanish-styled houses and manicured lawns.

"Who did you exploit today?" Sarah asked as Swan turned into his driveway.

"Huh? What does that mean?"

"Anyone who lives in a house this big must have exploited someone along the way."

"Look Ms. Sarah, sometimes people own things simply

because they've worked hard for them. I hope you'll understand that when you get older."

Sarah stood next to Swan as he turned the key to the front door. He stood frozen on the doorstep.

"Aren't you going to let me in?" she said. "I'd like to. I've only seen houses like this from the outside."

"Of course. Of course. It's just that I was thinking."

"Well, don't tax your brain."

Sarah walked past Swan and into the living room where she was surrounded by heavy, old English furniture that looked as if it had been dredged up from the Black Plague era.

"You actually live here?" she said, running her hand along the oak exterior of a large grandfather clock.

Swan remained rigid on the doorstep, peering in. He could suddenly envision his long-deceased grandmother quietly rocking in the wooden rocker next to the fireplace.

"When my books sold well," he said, "I bought this house. My mother's old now and when she's not down in Florida, likes to stay over. She's one of those snowbirds, you know. So I kind of decorated it with her in mind. She won't be around forever. Then I'll change the décor and make it more modern. I already have a decorator in mind."

Sarah smiled knowingly. "You're a good son. Do you think I can have a glass of wine?"

"Wine, really? Are you legal?"

"Of course I'm legal, Mr. Swan," Sarah said, smiling.

"OK, I'll take your word for it. White or red?"

"Anything."

Anything? Why did she keep saying that? It made him nervous.

He discovered a nice bottle of Beaujolais in a kitchen cupboard, prepared some crackers with cheese and olives, and returned triumphantly to the living room, only to find Sarah missing. She had vanished, leaving behind a bra, panties, socks, pants and shirt, strewn over a velvet wing-back chair.

"Oh my God." The words slithered out the corner of his mouth. "Oh my God."

In a panic, he called for her.

"Over here, in the bathroom," she said, and poked her blond head around from behind the door. "I thought I would freshen up a bit. All this grime from the crappy weather. If you don't mind, I'm going to take a shower."

Swan was speechless. *Freshen up?* He had heard the words spoken a million times before on TV shows. He knew exactly what that meant. Things were moving a little faster than he thought. Not that he minded, it's just that he wasn't used to it.

"Have you got like, a fresh towel, Mr. Swan? And maybe some sweats I can put on? My clothes are really wet and dirty."

By the time Swan found what Sarah wanted, she was already in the shower. He slinked into the bathroom, fully intending to place the stuff right on top of the toilet seat and then quickly leave. But once inside he found he couldn't help himself; the air was hot and steamy and Swan shaky with need. He leered at the moving body through the opaque shower curtains. Her breasts were perky, the nipples erect. A rich mound of blond hair protruded from between her thighs. This was no child he was looking at, this was a real woman.

Oh my God, thought Swan. A warm gush of desire ran through him. Had she seen him standing there? If so, and she did nothing, that would seal it. He would know what she wanted.

He remained a few more seconds and then decided to leave. There was no point pushing it ... they had all evening. He would let her get as comfortable as she needed.

Swan uncorked the wine and smelled it, souring his face. Wine wasn't his thing but he would force himself. He poured two glasses and set them down onto the coffee table in the living room. Then he munched hurriedly on some cheese and crackers and, with the evening's inevitable end in sight, popped a couple of Tic Tacs.

When Sarah emerged from the bathroom, her hair still wet, she announced she would like to take a nap. Twenty minutes, maybe half an hour. She was feeling a bit ragged and a short sleep would do her wonders. "Would you mind very much, Mr. Swan?" she said. "You're such a doll."

The pronouncement that he was a doll took Swan by surprise. He desperately wanted to take Sarah's damp head between his hands and kiss her. That was all he could think about. He was so close. But on the other hand, the fact she was feeling so comfortable with him that she could doze in his house, that was undoubtedly a good sign. A great sign. Not to mention that she was wearing his clothes! It all bespoke of something sensual and made Swan feel so good, like nothing he had experienced in a very long time.

Sarah raised the glass of wine to her nose and slowly smelled the bouquet, throwing her head back as if in ecstasy. She took a sip of the blood-red liquid and moaned. "So good," she said.

"I'm going to make the bed for you," said Swan nervously. "Wait right here." He ran upstairs. There was simply no way he would allow Sarah to sleep in his room; it was a pigsty, as usual, underwear and socks and magazines and bits of food all over his bed. Thank God his mother kept hers orderly. He put away into a dresser drawer the framed photos of his parents (his father now deceased) and plumped up the pillows. Ran his hands along the fluffy paisley comforter. Closed the frilly white curtains. It was lovely, really. All a woman like Sarah would want.

"Come up," he called out.

"Lovely," she said, peering into the bedroom.

With Sarah comfortable and the door closed, Swan stood outside the room and leaned against the wall. He contemplated slipping into bed and touching the nape of her slender neck, running his hands along her perfect body. He had a burning desire to make love to her, see her nipples standing erect, the feeling that would come over him would be exquisite. The naked women he often ogled in the magazines were pretty good, but a real one would even be better, he was certain of it. But for now, he would play it slow. Already the evening had transpired beyond his wildest expectations.

He had almost forgotten. He would need condoms. That's what everyone used. It was only a ten minute walk to the drugstore so Swan half-walked, half-ran. He envisioned Sarah in his arms, her eyelids fluttering under his caress. Ah yes, and he would ply her with glass after glass of red wine and even have some himself! To hell with tea biscuits!

Returning home, Swan gathered up Sarah's clothes, throwing them into the dryer. A gulp of wine gave him the courage to go into the bedroom and let his princess know he was back.

Swan's eyeballs wanted to flee their sockets—the bed was empty. He searched the house and called out for Sarah but she was nowhere to be found. He noticed that his mother's jewellery box, in which she kept her family heirlooms, was open and that various broaches, bracelets, pins, earrings, were gone.

In the bathroom, Swan splashed some water on his face. He looked in the mirror. He was gaunt, his eyes hollow, like he had been sick for a long time. "Oh, this is not good," he muttered to himself, his hands shaky.

He stood in the middle of the living room, not knowing what to do. For a brief moment, he thought about the lost jewellery but mostly he thought about how empty and cold the house was without Sarah in it. His eyes watered.

He walked mechanically to his bedroom on the third floor and started up the computer. He reread what he had written earlier and slumped his head onto the desk. Four lines. Four wretched lines. He had no talent, he knew that. He should give up writing, he really should.

It was then, with his head down, that Sarah came up behind him and put a hand on his shoulder, causing him to jump. There she stood, wearing the earrings, bracelets, and assorted jewellery Swan thought was gone.

"I would never steal from you, Mr. Swan," she said demurely. "You've been so nice to me. Finally I feel I have a home." She stood rocking back and forth on her heels, as if in a reverie. From her back pocket, she took out a knife. She remained silent and Swan was so overwhelmed that he too said nothing.

"I hate what I've become," she said quietly. She revealed that she hated her existence that depended on someone else bringing her to life. Living in the shadows, never fully realized.

"I don't know what you mean," Swan said.

"Doesn't matter. Here is a chance to set things right." She held the knife to her wrist.

"No, please don't," Swan said. "Maybe things are bad but they're never as bad as you think."

"That's easy for you to say, a successful author and all."

Swan exhaled and wiped his brow. "But I'm not. I just made all that stuff up. This isn't even my house—it belongs to my mother. You see, I'm a failure. I've never succeeded at anything."

"Huh, that's so interesting," Sarah said. "I know all that."

"You know all that?"

"Of course. I just wanted to hear it from you. You're not successful at all, and that's my problem."

"I still go on though. Now please give me that knife."

Sarah hesitated and then placed the knife in Swan's palm. "There," she said. "Maybe I don't need it. Maybe there's hope after all." She took off all the jewellery and put it onto the desk. "I hope we can start over."

"Of course I didn't think you would take anything. You're too honest for that. But, uh, well, why don't you have that nap and I'll fix you some food? We can both eat when you wake."

"That sounds amazing, Mr. Swan." She gave him a peck on the cheek. "There's just one more thing … uh, and you may not like it. Well, actually, you may not believe it."

"How much worse can it be than a knife? You hurting yourself? How much worse? Not much, I can tell you."

"OK, well, Mr. Swan, it's like this. I've been waiting a long time for you."

"Waiting a long time? What do you mean?"

"Well, I hung out on your porch, sometimes in your garage. But mostly I walked a lot, I just kept on walking. Aimless walking you could say. I kept thinking you would write me back into your stories, but you always had trouble. You had 'writer's block' or something. Once you almost brought me fully to life, like when you started that story about a young girl who had trouble with her boyfriend, the same boyfriend who kicked her out of his moving car. That was me. You brought me into the world but then didn't finish. So I went back to just hanging around, waiting."

"WHAT? Are you nuts?"

"I got tired of waiting for you, Mr. Swan. So I went downtown a few times. Sometimes I even followed you when you yourself went downtown. A lot of times you took the subway so it was easy to follow you. I'm pretty good at slipping past things, I didn't even pay to take the subway."

Swan looked at Sarah with genuine fright in his eyes. "What do you want?" he muttered.

"I just want you to write me fully into existence. I want to be a fully-realized character. You started me and now that I have a taste for life, I want more. It's hard to exist in the margins, you know. Sometimes I struggle for a breath, my body shakes."

One of his characters? So that's who she was. He got it now ... well, sort of. Kind of. "I hope you're telling me the truth."

"I am. I am."

"Really? Why should I believe you?"

"How would I know about the guy who kicked his

girlfriend out of the car? It's not a published story. There's only one way."

"My God, you're right," he said, shaking his head. "Ok, ok, but I'm not a very good writer. You must have been waiting a very long time. That story, the one I didn't finish, the one about you, it's so old."

Swan kept on shaking his head. "Responsibility, responsibility," he said. "I don't know if I have it in me."

"That's because you give up too easily, Mr. Swan. You should write a complete first draft, even if it's crappy. Then rewrite. Most good writing comes from rewriting."

"You have a point."

"And give me a last name please."

"I can try I guess."

"Just use your imagination, Mr. Swan. Free and easy. Don't be afraid. It's not that hard."

"Right."

"Just believe in yourself."

Swan lowered his eyes and nodded slowly.

"Now I'm going to take that nap. I've been feeling a bit dizzy."

In the kitchen, Swan fixed salad and grilled cheese sandwiches, which he would re-heat when Sarah woke. For dessert, there was cheesecake. This was better, much better. He breathed easier. Maybe Sarah could stay for awhile. He wasn't sure how she was at doing the laundry or cleaning or ironing, but he could show her how it was done. Best of all, she could even do the cooking; he didn't mind preparing the food this one occasion, it was real special.

Once he had finished, Swan ran back up the stairs and looked in his mother's bedroom. Sarah wasn't there and the sheets looked undisturbed. He breathed deeply. Went into his bedroom and sat down at his computer. He looked at the few lines he had written earlier that day and bore in mind what Sarah had told him, that most good writing comes from rewriting. That all he had to do was write a first draft. Those lines were salvageable, he now realized.

He began. One word at a time. Like old faithful friends, characters that had existed only in his mind started springing to life. Including Sarah Thomas, the young woman who had given him renewed hope. He would now tell her story.

GROTESQUE

NOT TEN MINUTES after settling in his favourite armchair to watch back-to-back episodes of *Leave it to Beaver*, Nathan Mandelbaum heard a scream that shook him out of his TV-induced stupor. It was a scream so strange, so unlike anything he had ever heard, that he dropped his bag of M & M's and ran to the kitchen door, which overlooked his backyard.

The back of his tiny house bordered on a ravine and Nathan sometimes saw squirrels and raccoons. The odd rabbit and even a coyote or two. He often left food out for the critters. But on this particular day, it was no animal, nothing he had ever seen before. The sight of this … this thing, so unnerved Nathan that he immediately locked the back door and withdrew a few steps into his kitchen, his heart beating rapidly.

That night, while lying in bed, he heard the same scream again. It reminded Nathan of the unearthly screams that the bloodthirsty creature in the horror movie

Scream of the Banshee emitted. Guttural, as if it emanated from the bowels of hell itself.

The next morning when he arrived at his work as an insurance claims examiner, Nathan found that he had thirty-six e-mails and eleven phone messages waiting for him. "I take a mental health day and look what I get," he thought to himself. Doris Camilleri was upset with him because her car had been repaired with after-market parts. Max Mandelbaum (no relation) cursed him out for depreciating his stolen leather jacket. Chris Norton roared because the carpet in his basement was wet with sewer backup water and hadn't yet been replaced. Karen Simpson complained that she now had mismatched shingles following the repair of her roof.

Nathan's eyes zig-zagged across his computer screen as he surveyed the damage. "A lot of upset customers," he thought. "Screw them. They upset my life, and I don't deserve that." He took a long sip of his double-double coffee and a hard bite of his jelly donut, squirting red sticky liquid onto the back of his hand.

"Hey bud. Missed you Thursday." It was his pal, Ron Teegarden. If truth be known, Ron was one of the very people he could tolerate. With mutual interests in the paranormal and with equal doses of cynicism and a disdain for most people, fashion and fitness and popular culture, they were fast friends.

Nathan licked the jelly off his hand. "Listen Ron, we have to do lunch today. I have something important to tell you."

And so over lunch of grilled cheese sandwiches, chicken fingers and fries at a local diner, Nathan revealed what had been percolating in his brain since the previous evening.

"Ron, you won't believe what I'm going to tell you," he said, "but I saw the strangest thing in my backyard."

"I'm all ears, my friend. So what do you mean by *strange*?"

But Nathan wasn't listening. His attention had suddenly been diverted by an old woman with her hair in curlers sitting at the counter.

"Would you look at that," he said, pointing with his forefinger. "You'd think she'd have the decency to take those stupid things off before going out."

"This isn't her bedroom," Ron said.

"Exactly. And what about the guy sitting in the booth behind us," Nathan whispered. "He's whistling through his nose. It's totally disgusting."

There was the goth girl with her black makeup ("complete stoner otherwise she'd realize how ridiculous she looks") the construction worker with his hard hat still on ("what barn was he raised in?") the students carrying their books ("they're idiots if they think they're going to change the world with worthless garden-variety psychology degrees"). After the two men had had their fill of denigrating the other patrons in the diner, they returned to the subject at hand.

"This thing in the backyard ... " Nathan said. He stopped, breathless, and collected himself. "It was unreal. It was a creature of some sort, eating the chicken I put out."

"*Creature?* Are you kidding?"

"I'm telling you, a creature. A *Goddamn creature*. It had little ummm ... wings. About three feet in height, I'm guessing. It was bent over eating so I couldn't tell for sure. But she had a human face, sort of, that I could see."

"What do you mean *sort of*? That's pretty vague."

"Of course it's vague, dumbo. That's why I said it."

Ron threw a French fry, hitting Nathan in the forehead.

"Do that again and I'll kill you," Nathan said, staring daggers.

"Ok, fine. Relax," Ron said, smirking. "Anyway, you said it was a woman?"

"Well, she had these small gross breasts, just hanging down. And long stringy black hair, all matted."

Ron drummed his fork on the table. "I don't know, Nate," he said slowly and deliberately. "That's, you know, pretty far-fetched."

"It was there, Ron, in black and white. I'm not lying. These tiny legs and tiny arms and … wings. It gave me the creeps I'll tell you—just a freak of nature."

Nathan tried to assuage Ron's scepticism by telling him about the unearthly screams that came from the creature.

"Ok, better. But still … "

"You know when that thing was eating, there weren't any animals around. All the birds and squirrels had taken a hike."

"Hey, maybe it was a chupacabra," Ron said. "They're supposed to be about three feet in height."

"The thing that sucks the blood out of animals? They're down in Mexico and Puerto Rico, not Toronto."

"What about the Jersey Devil? They're known to have wings."

"Don't be so lame. We're talking New Jersey, right. And we're living in Toronto, get it?"

Ron went through a list of possible suspects—pixies, fairies, elves, sprites, brownies, gnomes, leprechauns, harpies, wood nymphs—and Nathan discounted each and every one, getting more and more upset with each suggestion.

After they had exhausted every possibility, including a deformed human, they settled on the one thing it had to be —*a fallen angel*.

"That's got to be it, Ron," Nathan said. "Like, you and me are pretty rebellious guys, don't you think?"

"I would agree with that."

"And fallen angels are rebellious angels that have been booted from heaven."

"Maybe she's come to visit us," Ron said.

"Makes sense."

"The question is," Ron asked, now into his second piece of apple pie, "what are you going to do about it?"

Nathan appeared nonplussed and thumped his chest in a grandiose manner. "I'm going to go capture her," he said matter-of-factly.

After work that evening, Nathan went to an army surplus store and bought a pair of Russian-made night-vision goggles for $499.00. He was told they were the real deal, able to gather ambient light in the form of moonlight and transform images into a clear green hued re-creation of the scene he was observing. The next day he had a motion detector installed above his backyard door and the day following a camera that took pictures every thirty seconds.

Although he hadn't told Ron, he knew that the sighting of the creature was a watershed moment in his life, a turning point. There was a reason why the angel had come into his backyard and Nathan knew that if he found her (and had proof of her existence), his life would never be the same. He didn't know exactly how it would change, he just knew it would.

For the next week, each morning before he left for work, Nathan made sure to sprinkle chicken pieces in the backyard, along with peanut butter smeared on crackers, bits of chocolate chip cookies, a boiled sweet potato, and apple quarters. It was a grand feast but he figured it was worth it, since he had no idea what fallen angels liked to eat.

But after a week, there was no sight of the angel. All the food was gone though and as he scanned the camera, he saw blue jays, lots of squirrels, little brown birds, a couple of raccoons, one skunk, a few crows, but no angel.

"I haven't seen her," he told Ron in frustration, "and it's costing me a fortune. Plus my next door neighbour is getting pretty upset ... she tells me that all the food is attracting raccoons."

"You never cared about your neighbours before."

"And I still don't. She's a twit. But I'd rather she didn't talk to me at all."

Nathan told Ron he'd have to go into the ravine to search.

"She'd be living alone, maybe in a cave or something," Ron said.

"There aren't any caves there. It's a ravine." He couldn't be sure but he thought he saw Ron snicker as the latter returned to his desk.

Hiking boots, a flashlight, khaki shorts, a walking stick whittled out of an oak tree branch, night-vision goggles, backpack, insect repellent, water bottle. He found an ancient army vest in his closet that he had long forgotten about; it was replete with deep pockets, perfect for carrying the various paraphernalia that he was taking on his journey, but he couldn't get it to button around his substantial girth. Perhaps most important, he took along a large burlap sack in which to snag the fallen angel.

Nathan knew that he would have to make the journey through the ravine at night, that he stood a better chance of finding the fallen angel then. A gut feeling.

The ravine was fairly well-traveled by experienced hikers, but by and large difficult, wild, home to the occasional coyote, raccoons, skunks, field mice and the like. Nathan had been in there once before but found the going too rough, the undulations too steep, the landscape full of burrs and thorny shrubs, thick berry bushes and jagged rocks. It was in fact a small forest in the heart of the city.

It had rained the previous day and the ground was full of earthworms. Every step he took, Nathan squashed one or two, exploding out from the underside of his heavy boots. Moreover, despite the fact it was April, it was cold and damp inside the ravine and almost immediately he regretted the fact that he had worn shorts. "Bad choice," he said to himself.

He affixed the night-vision goggles onto his head, leaving the lens parked on his forehead. For the moment, he would rely on his flashlight. A steady beam of light cut a narrow swath through the darkness. He could hear cars motoring so he knew the street was fairly close at hand;

should he lose his way, he could easily veer out of the ravine back into the urban jungle.

As he moved along, using his walking stick to manipulate past the bushes and plants that crept up in his path, he breathed in the clear, sweet smells of the water-logged woods ... spruce trees, grass, pine nuts and a whole host of others that he couldn't identify. The thicket was dense and burrs stuck to his clothes. His exposed legs became cold and scratched.

He came across what looked like a giant concrete culvert, the overpass of which was a footpath covered in grass. Nathan thought it might have been a sewer line at one point. He walked the outside length of it and figured that it was about twenty yards in total. He peered inside but it was pitch black and he could see nothing. This was a job for his expensive goggles. He parked the flashlight into his vest pocket and lowered the goggles from his forehead onto his eyes. A green world emerged as he ventured in, crouching as he went. There was a wretched acrid smell, like rotting fish and urine. And all he could see however were piles of rocks, like glowing kryptonite.

Suddenly something made an angry beeline toward him. He could see it, this green raging thing, wings flailing. Nathan screamed and ran out backwards, hitting his head at the edge of the concrete as he emerged. He continued running and didn't look back, tripping once or twice.

After a few minutes he stopped and collected his breath. He dropped to one knee and ran his hand along his sore head. "Fuck," he said, out of breath. "Now she's in for it."

He knew he had to go back and get her. The grass was tall and he used his walking stick like a scythe, cutting a path. And then he was there, standing a few feet from the culvert opening once again. But he couldn't bring himself to go back in.

It didn't matter though because, as soon as Nathan tentatively stuck his head into the opening of the pipe, the angel came hurtling toward him once again. As if by instinct, he took his walking stick and used it like a Kendo Stick, whacking the creature across the stomach and doubling it over. Then he reared back and smashed the angel's back, once, twice.

He shone his flashlight and then pushed at the prone thing with his boot. More animal than human, it was strikingly grotesque. A black beak, small beady eyes, and hair cascading along both pointed ears. It had human-like legs except the feet resembled those of a chicken. Beneath the wings were appendages, stick-like arms, which ended in claws. And those breasts!

Nathan manoeuvred the angel into the burlap sack and lifted it up onto his shoulder. He was a big guy at two hundred and thirty pounds and the sack felt surprisingly light. Walking through the forest, he grew fearful of the intangible dark shapes that surrounded him in the night, imagining they were stalking him. "Save your threats," he whispered hoarsely. "I'm taking her. Nothing can be done."

Back at the house, he opened the garage door and carefully placed the sack on the ground. Then he pulled it open. The angel was still unconscious and now, in the full light, the sight of her made him wince—for there seemed to be what looked like a half-eaten bat stuck beneath her beak, fully-ensconced within the thing's mouth. And the smell that emanated from her, like rotten eggs, made him feel like retching.

He put on a pair of gloves and propped the angel against a wall. He needed time to think. It dawned on him that he could put the damned thing into a cage. He had a very old dog carrier in a corner of the garage, used for his German Sheppard dog Roxie, long since deceased. That would do.

Nathan carried the angel and deposited her into the cage. He carefully removed the bat from its mouth and then locked the door, securing the plastic latch with twine. He looked into the carrier and saw that his catch was coming to life, fluttering her eyes. He stayed, fascinated, holding his nose with one hand and running his hand along the bars with the other, prodding her to wake. And when she did, the snarl she gave out so frightened Nathan that he nearly tumbled over backwards.

"Fuck you," Nathan said. "You won't be getting out anytime soon."

The good thing was that this freak of nature was at his mercy. She couldn't stand up in the carrier and try as she might to rattle the bars, they wouldn't give. All of which meant that he could do what he wanted. Which played right into the plan, now percolating in his brain. As he had previously thought, catching the angel would be a turning point in his life. Now he knew why; he would put the freak on display and charge people money. It was the perfect plan, the one way out of his miserable job. He'd be his own boss. Never again would he have to answer to anyone. Screw 'em all.

Early the next morning he called in sick to work. The angel was crazy, shaking the carrier with ferocity, screaming, screaming.

"Shut it," Nathan said. "You belong to me now."

He took a picture of the angel with his phone and posted it on Facebook. He sent the same photo to a crypto-zoologist he had once heard on that late-night radio show of the paranormal. He also took out a half-page ad in local community newspapers. He even called the Biology Department at the University of Toronto to let them know of his unique find.

Word spread quickly and in no time at all, Nathan's phone was ringing incessantly. His plan was starting to take hold. He would open up his garage door three days from now so that everyone could have a look at the creature. And he, Nathan Mandelbaum, would be the carnival barker. Twenty dollars a head, that seemed about right. Even a bit cheap considering the enormity of his find. How much would people pay to see Nessie, or Bigfoot?

As he sat at his computer, Nathan realized that the fallen angel had become the single most important thing in his life. His heart leapt and he pumped his right fist maniacally into the air. "Yes! Yes!" It had all come down to this and he had to do everything right. For one, he wouldn't call or text Ron—his friend would only get in the way, maybe even want a cut of the proceeds. He was better off alone.

He stood up and did some deep knee bends; his joints creaked and after three such bends, he had a hard time righting himself. But if there was one other thing that made him uncomfortable, it was the constant uneasiness that plagued him. It led to a certain ennui, as if he always knew that things would never get better. Why try to right things then? He knew he wasn't very good-looking, a *schlub* as his mother used to sometimes call him before she passed, a Yiddish term for a big, clumsy oaf. Well, he was grossly overweight, and his face pock-marked from old acne scars. Women showed no interest in him, except they always marvelled at his size fourteen shoes. At the young age of thirty-two, his vitality had been fully zapped.

He could hear the angel making a racket and realized that he had better feed her. He gathered food that he had in the fridge and cupboards and deposited them all into a big bowl—chicken, pastrami, salami, croutons, whole-wheat bread, chocolate chip cookies. In the garage, he raised his voice and ordered the angel to pipe down, shaking his walking stick menacingly at her. As unlikely as it seemed, she moved to the very back of the carrier and as soon as she did, Nathan quickly removed the twine and undid the latch. The angel snatched at the bowl and started eating. Food crumbs cascaded down her face and onto her chest, nestling in her breasts.

Nathan watched in awe as the angel ate with its claws, tearing up the chicken. "What a goddamn freak," he thought. "No wonder God kicked you out." He rattled the bars with his walking stick and pointed to the bowl of water he had placed next to the food. "Drink," he said. "You need to be hydrated for when everyone comes."

Over the next few days, Nathan continued to call in sick to work. Ron phoned to enquire about his absence but he simply told his friend that he wasn't well, that was all. A bald-faced lie but it didn't matter that he wouldn't tell his best friend the truth. Now it was all about him, Nathan, carnival barker.

The day before the big unveiling, religious zealots demonstrated in front of Nathan's house. They held placards that said that the angel's appearance was a sign from a very angry God that the world was coming to an end. They quoted biblical scriptures. Verses from *Luke* and *Matthew*. One in particular caught Nathan's attention: *So it will be at the end of the age; the angels will come forth and take out the wicked from among the righteous ... Matthew 13:49.* Nathan wondered where he fit into the scheme of things—a wicked person, or a righteous one? It didn't matter; it was all crap.

Nathan watched from an opening in the curtains in his living room. He would have liked to pummel the bible thumpers but realized they were good for the entertainment value. He fully expected more like them the next day, the lunatic fringe, people with wild interpretations of his find. What he also expected was another call from his best friend, which was exactly what he got. Nathan let it ring through to his answering machine.

"Asshole! You tell me you're sick but the truth is you've been harbouring that angel you told me about. I read about it, heard it on the radio. I won't forget this, Nathan. I won't forget it one little bit. And one last thing, buddy. Your little ruse will be found out. There ain't no fallen angel, there's just you dressing up some little person, a midget or something, in a costume. Wings, yah right."

At 7:30 the next morning, a line of people snaked around the block, waiting for a glimpse of the angel. There were TV crews with their cameras, radio personalities, kids on skateboards, moms pushing strollers, old men with canes, even an ice cream vendor who parked his truck at the curbside, right next to the hot dog vendor. The event was supposed to start at 9 am sharp but Nathan came out early to set up, bringing with him a large coffee and a couple of bran muffins. He taped a large cardboard sign on the garage door advising that every customer had exactly one minute alone with the angel. He also wrote $20.00 all over the sign. Then he set up a folding chair in front of the garage and plunked his large frame in it. He had been to the bank the day before and had plenty of money to make change.

The line got progressively longer and the TV crews and radio personalities vied for an interview with him. He told his story over and over again, embellishing it by saying he had come across it in a cave in a remote region of Algonquin Park, adding that it had been a life-or-death struggle with the angel ... it definitely did not want to be taken alive. He had emerged victorious, but bruised and bloody.

It was already hot at this early morning and Nathan was feeling the heat; drops of perspiration dotted his forehead and his armpits were dripping. But true to his word, at exactly 9 am, he opened the garage door and let the first person in. He set a timer to one minute and waited. Not long as it turned out, for that first person, a middle-aged woman, ran out screaming in just a few seconds: "Oh my God, oh my God!"

That reaction was better than Nathan could have hoped. He collected twenty dollars from the next person, and waited for a similar reaction. He got it too. The young boy came out with his hand over his mouth, as if he was about to vomit.

"It's perfect," Nathan thought. "Just throw up now."

"Mister, that thing is ugly as shit," the kid said.

"Tell everyone, kid."

And so it went. All day long. By noon, Nathan had to get a small box from the garage to store all the money. If the reactions he was getting from customers was what he wanted, so too was the reaction he got from the angel. It hissed at each and every person who entered, sometimes screaming so wickedly that a few people fainted right in the garage. Nathan simply doused the fallen person with water from a garden hose and dragged them out.

"Another fallen person!" he yelled out to the crowd.

At 4 pm, Nathan had had enough and shouted to the gathered crowds that he was shutting down, to come back the following day. Then he slid the garage door closed, locked it, and stood with his large arms crossed against his chest, like he was guarding national secrets.

On the second day, a couple of special interest groups showed up — AETA (the Association of Ethical Treatment of Animals) and PDD (People with Disabilities against Discrimination). Both groups were aghast and demanded that Nathan let the angel go. "It's a wild animal," a spokesperson from AETA said. "It's a disabled woman," a spokesperson from PDD said. A First-Nations group turned up as well, telling Nathan that the angel belonged back in Algonquin, with her own kind. "Bad things will happen to you if you interfere with nature," they said.

Superstitious idiots, Nathan thought. In fact, he ignored anyone who offered any advice. There were simply too many people who wanted to see the angel, too much money to be had.

The same scene repeated itself for the next few days. As was expected, Ron showed up. He wanted to see the angel without paying. "I'll blackmail you," he said. "Tell everyone that it's just a midget dressed up." Nathan, considerably larger than Ron, bodily dragged his old friend to the street and threw him to the ground. "Get out, asshole. And don't come back! You're not welcome."

"You make me sick!"

"I only became your friend because I felt sorry for you," Nathan said, and for good measure he spat at Ron.

Every night Nathan counted his cash before going to sleep. It was unbelievable how much was coming in. He had plenty so thought nothing of hiring a guard to stand in front of the garage every night, in case someone got any funny ideas about breaking in. And it all kept coming, more and more money, especially after numerous pictures of the angel were posted on social media sites and in the newspapers. The lineups to see the angel grew larger each day.

But on the fifth day, Nathan woke in the middle of the night. He was really too excited to sleep and from his bed, turned on the TV. Suddenly, the entire bedroom was irradiated from the bluish light from the set. He watched *The Bourne Identity* for awhile but his concentration waned. He kept thinking about all the things he could do with his money. For some reason, he muted the volume. And it was then that he became aware that the angel was inordinately quiet. Throughout much of every night and early each morning, it put up a terrible clatter, squawking and screaming. He sat straight up in his bed and strained his ears, but there were no sounds. Not a peep. It was four in the morning and Nathan ran through his house to the garage, where he saw that the angel was not moving. He poked at it with his walking stick but it remained inert. It struck him just then that with all the turmoil the past few days, that he had forgotten to feed the angel.

Nathan sat down in front of the dog carrier on a milk crate and looked in at the dead thing. A large pool of blood was slowly seeping out the crate onto the floor. *Oh shit,* he thought. *I'm ruined.* He felt sick to his stomach. Dizzy from lack of sleep, his head swirled. It was odd and didn't make much sense, but Nathan suddenly started to wonder about the angel. Where she had actually come from, whether she had parents, friends even. Her own kind might have been missing her.

I wonder if she was an anomaly, just a misfit, he thought sadly. *Kind of like me. Christ, and I failed her.* A lump developed in his throat and a few tears ran down his cheeks. It was so uncharacteristic of him but once the tears started, they just wouldn't stop. He sat there a long time, not moving, his face wet, a contorted mess.

"You in there, sir?" He heard three knocks on the garage door.

"Yes, it's me. Thank you. Just checking on the angel."

After sitting and weeping for quite some time, Nathan realized there was only one thing left to do. He lifted the dog carrier up and took it into his house and through the back door in his kitchen, where he slipped into the ravine. He walked to where he had found the angel in the abandoned pipe, and set the carrier down, catching his breath. He looked at his watch and realized that the early-birds would be lining up just at this time, right outside his garage.

He started digging a hole in the ground with his hands, with the heels of his shoes, and with a sharp rock. He worked at it until the hole was quite deep and then took the angel from the carrier and gently placed her down. Then he covered her up with the dirt.

"I really hope you're at peace now," he whispered. "And I'm sorry. I didn't mean for it to go this way."

He walked slowly back to his house, where he paid the security guard and then told him he could go, he was no longer needed. His hands filthy, covered in blood, he took down the cardboard sign that still adorned the garage door. Then he told everyone in line that the show was over, the angel was no longer, she had passed away during the night. As proof, he slid open the garage door. And he stood in front of the garage all day long, saying the same thing over and over again, that there was nothing left to see. Reporters asked for interviews but he would not grant them at this time, telling them he would give one statement when he was ready. The crowds dwindled and Nathan retired into his house. A few people tried to open the garage door, unsuccessfully.

⚭

Over the next few days, something slowly and inexorably changed in Nathan. He quit his insurance job and took a volunteer assignment as a recreation program assistant at a community centre. He felt the new person that was emerging from him like a physical sensation; his skin tingled when he played basketball games with the kids at the centre.

Back at home, he cleaned his house for the first time in many years, the very house his mother had bequeathed to him. He scrubbed the kitchen sink, dusted, and removed all the cobwebs that had collected over the years. And in front of the house he deposited all the junk he had accumulated over the years. His old treasures, now worthless, ready for the garbage pick-up. It took him days but when he was through, he walked through the house and saw the remarkable change. And as he sat down to relax, the first time he had been able to do so in quite some time, he realized that he wasn't exactly sure what he would do with his life, where he would go, how he would live. Moreover, how he would overcome the fears and inadequacies that dominated his essence, that turned up day after day after day and defined him. He only knew that he couldn't go back to being the person he once was, it was dead and buried, like the fallen angel. Like the freak he had once been.

BUTTERFLY DREAMS

ASHTON TURNED THE key in the door lock of the apartment he once lived in and let himself in. Like a bear after a long winter, something stirred in him five weeks earlier and he felt compelled to spy on his ex-girlfriend. Knowing she would be at work, he crept in every Tuesday morning at 10, making himself at home in Evie's apartment, the place she now shared with the man who had replaced Ashton.

A year had passed since the breakup, one that, while certainly not Ashton's idea, had been more or less amicable. It was for that reason that Evie never changed the locks. But why exactly he devised this plan was something only he knew; it might have had something to do with getting back at the woman who spurned him, making him feel he had the upper hand. Certainly he never felt that way during the entire time he was going out with Evie. She liked him, she had said, but he wasn't husband material. No job, no ambition, those were the problems.

Each time Ashton ate a bit of food, not much, not enough to arouse suspicion, usually a grilled cheese sandwich, or one of prepared meats, pastrami, salami, and the like, making sure to wash the dishes and put everything back in place. He would then pour himself a half glass of red wine and settle down on the black leather sofa to watch TV.

The first time he entered, Ashton was especially careful not to disturb anything. But now, after four weeks, he was growing restless and tended to look upon the affair as a bit of a game. The object of which, he determined in his fiendish mind, was to take something, a small item that might go unnoticed. Like a spare toothbrush, amongst the many Evie kept in a glass.

He stuck the toothbrush in his pocket and wandered about the living room. All of his framed photos had been replaced by pictures of Evie's new beau. *Not as handsome as I would have imagined*, thought Ashton. He considered putting a small scratch on the glass of the frame using his penknife, obscuring the man's face, but figured that would definitely be noticed.

In week five, Ashton popped a button on one of Evie's blouses. When he arrived at his own apartment, he put it next to the toothbrush.

In week six, Ashton snipped a couple of broad green leaves from a plant.

In week seven, he took something bigger—a hard cover book with plenty of photos entitled *The Rebuilding of London after The Great Fire*. That was a gamble, he knew, because books generally don't go missing and people with substantial collections know what they have. Especially large-format picture books. But he figured that the many books Evie and her partner had would work to his advantage—the detestable lovebirds had so many books, most of which were Evie's, that it was unlikely that a single missing book would elicit any suspicion. And if it did, well ... so what? Perhaps that might become an area of contention between the happy couple. Besides, he always liked that particular book, had read through it a number of times while he and Evie had been a couple, and considered it at least half his own.

He contemplated what his next theft might be. But instead of stealing, he elected to introduce something into the apartment from the outside. That would raise the stakes and seemed more fun. The first item he brought in was a book, sticking it into the bookcase. Then a wine glass, exactly similar to the ones that were in the kitchen closet, Instead of six, now Evie had seven sparkling wine glasses.

He realized the wine glass was a bold move so he toned down his next item—an unopened package of dental floss that he stuck in a bathroom drawer. A pen, eraser, pencil, nail clipper, bottle of aspirin, bar of soap ... a whole secret universe did he bring in, making sure that all the items were similar to what was already in the apartment.

As he lay sprawled on the couch one Tuesday morning, completely sated with his ingenuity, he downed a shotglass of Jack Daniels and munched on a piece of Gorgonzola cheese. But as the food went down heavily, causing a bit of heartburn, he thought that perhaps it was all too simple, without intrigue. Inert objects were one thing, but living things were a cut above. Yes, he needed to bring in something live.

So the following week, on a Monday morning, he captured a Monarch butterfly in a glass jar in the middle of a public park. It was the summer and kids abounded; his crazed lunging after the flying insect brought a lot of finger-pointing and stares.

"I'm a scientist at the U of T," he said to the bewildered children and parents who had gathered round. "And I'm taking this butterfly for a science experiment. But don't worry, it won't be hurt."

"Promise, mister?" a little girl with blond pigtails said. She was on the verge of tears.

"Cross my heart," he said, holding the jar up in the air so the girl could see the butterfly. "See the little holes in the lid? That's so that it can breathe properly. And the grass at the bottom is food, what they like to eat."

"What's the nature of the experiment?" the mother of the little girl asked.

"It has to do with climate change. We allow different insects to fly around in different environments and see how that affects their core temperatures. It's interesting work, very safe for the butterflies, and then we set them free."

"Interesting."

"Yes, interesting," the little girl said. "Don't forget to feed them leaves. They like leaves."

That night, he watched the butterfly, making sure it didn't die. He slept not a wink and in the morning hightailed it to Evie's, where he let it loose. It fluttered about for a time and came to rest at the top of the bookcase. There it silently stayed, its wings beating slowly. Ashton opened the window a crack—that would explain how it got in. And hopefully the dumb butterfly wouldn't fly out. But knowing that Evie was a real stickler for shutting all the windows, unplugging all the appliances and double-checking that the front door was locked before leaving the apartment, she would blame her current boyfriend. That was perfect, just what he was hoping. It was a great day, the best he'd had in the apartment so far.

Often while Ashton was at Evie's, the phone would ring. Annoying telemarketers. They would always hang up once the answering machine picked up. With each call, Ashton would put his feet up on the coffee table, close his eyes, and imagine that it was Evie calling:

"Hello?"

"Evie, you called!"

"Well, you know, I figured it out. The butterfly gave it away. Only you would be that clever."

"You're pretty smart yourself."

"Thanks. How're you enjoying the apartment anyway?"

"Fine. Taking a bath right now. Using some of your bath salts. Hope you don't mind. But, uh, aside from that, I see you've taken down all my pictures."

"Well, you know. Matt and all."

"*Matt*? Never pictured you with a *Matt*. So, on to the point: why are you calling, Evie?"

"Well, you know, it's like this. I think I made a big mistake. I haven't been happy with Matt from the get-go and maybe, just maybe, it has to do with the fact that I never really got over you."

"It's been getting worse, has it?"

"Definitely."

"Look Evie, I hate to tell you this but I've moved on."

"You have?"

"Ahh, just kidding! Why don't you get yourself back to your apartment and join me in this here bath? I'll keep the water hot. Just hurry."

The week after he brought in the butterfly, it was nowhere to be seen. Ashton checked throughout the apartment, even looking in the garbage, but it was gone. The window was also closed. He made himself a peanut butter and jam sandwich and settled down to watch the daytime soap *The Young and the Restless* when the doorbell rang. He quickly lowered the volume to a whisper and waited breathlessly.

The doorbell rang on insistently, getting Ashton's heart muscle contracting so fast he was certain the person on the other side could hear the beating.

"Hello!" The voice was sweet and female. Not Evie's.

Ashton crept to the front door and peered through the peephole.

"Are you there?"

It was at that very instant, the very second that he heard the melodious whisper of 'are you there?' that a flood of unreason overtook Ashton, as if the neurotransmitters between brain cells suddenly snapped, and he found himself mechanically turning the door knob.

He lightly shook the hirsute hand that was extended to him. The hand was connected to an arm that was overgrown with what looked like black weeds. There was no question about it: The person standing opposite him was the hairiest woman Ashton had ever seen. She was also extraordinarily large; he estimated her eight at not an ounce less than two hundred fifty pounds or one and a half versions of himself.

The woman kept on pumping Ashton's hand. "I'm Susan Horvath," she said, enthusiastically. "Your new next door neighbour. Just moved in last week. Thought I'd introduce myself and bring you a pie I made. Apple crumble."

Ashton cautiously grabbed hold of the pie, glad to be out of Susan's grasp. He remained mute, unsmiling.

"And you are?" Susan said, waving her plump hand in little circles.

Ashton slowly came out of his reverie. "And I'm Matt." he said tentatively.

"Well, nice to meet you, Matt. I'm sure we'll be seeing a lot more of each other. I'm off to work in just a few minutes."

And with those parting words, Susan ambled down the hallway to her apartment. Ashton carried the pie, which now felt as heavy as a sack of potatoes, into the living room and slumped into a chair. What had he done? He was ruined, there was no doubt. Maybe he could go to London —he had heard it was nice there in the spring. Besides, they had built it up quite nicely after the fire, or so he read.

Ashton held onto his head and tried to consider his options, but it was no use. He couldn't think, couldn't bring forth a single coherent thought. He shut the TV, put the pie in a bag and quickly left the apartment.

That night Ashton paced his apartment like a caged animal. His body felt taut and his mind raced. The shock of the morning had still not dissipated. He drank a tall glass of Drambuie to settle down ... then a second. A warm glow enveloped him. Whatever he was going to do, he had to do it fast, that much he knew.

As the evening drained away, Ashton's anxiety gave way to desperate exhilaration. Yes, he could do it. He was starting to figure out, well, sort of. For a fleeting moment, he thought that the truth might be his way out but then … no. Whoever said the truth would set you free was full of shit. It would only make things a lot worse, of that Ashton was certain. There really was only one way out: Keep Susan away from Evie and the real Matt.

He hadn't eaten all day. He cut a large slice of Susan's pie and gobbled it down. Then a second piece. The sugar rush made him giddy and he chuckled at his half-baked plans. He took a long slug of Drambuie straight from the bottle and stumbled into bed with his clothes still on, falling fast asleep.

At precisely 8 the next morning, Ashton sat in his ten-year-old Toyota Corolla and sipped on a diet coke. He knew that Evie usually left for work at 8:15. If all went as planned, she would leave with Matt, although that was no certainty.

When Evie appeared, Ashton slouched down. He had parked a good distance from the building; he couldn't take the chance of being spotted. Unfortunately, she was alone. He watched her walk around the block and then scooted into the building. Hopefully he wouldn't run into Matt but as the two had only seen each other in photos, chances were slim there'd be any recognition, especially if he kept his head low.

He checked the mailboxes—there it was: Susan Horvath. Apt. 602. Fat Susan Horvath, she of the bountiful hair. How could a woman grow a better moustache than him? But she made exquisite pie, that much he would give her. He buzzed and waited. Nothing. This part he hadn't anticipated. He returned to his car, found a pad and pen and began writing:

> *Susan: Something very important to discuss with you. This is <u>really urgent</u>. We must talk today. My home # is 647-1829. <u>Under no circumstances knock on my door!</u> I'll explain later.*
> *Matt*

Back in the building he waited for someone to let him in and then bolted the six floors to Susan's apartment where he stood outside and listened, his heart thumping. He knocked softly but there was no answer so he slipped the note into the crack of the door.

When the phone rang at 6:10 that evening, it came not a moment too soon for Ashton. He bolted to the phone. Susan!

"I called as soon as I read your note," she said. "Is everything alright?"

"Peachy. I wanted to tell you that you make the most exquisite pie.

"Thanks!"

"Look, there's something I need to talk to you about. Where can we meet?"

"You mean tonight?

"As soon as possible."

"Wow, sounds important. Well, I'll just come down the hall right now."

"No, no! Not my place. Let's meet somewhere neutral, if you don't mind."

"I don't mind. Give me half an hour."

At 6:45, Ashton met Susan at Starbuck's, far removed from where she lived. He explained to her that his life was in a state of turmoil because he was caring for ailing parents (his mother was ill with MS; his father with Parkinson's), but that when he met her, it was if a ray of divine light shone down upon him. Her generosity with the pie was unparalleled. He realized that he needed to spend time with someone. Her, Susan Horvath.

"I can appreciate that you're going through a tough time, Matt. But we don't really know each other."

"So we'll get to know each other, it's no big deal. Every relationship starts somewhere, even from a very innocuous beginning. Like from a single apple pie."

"Apple crumble, to be exact. But are asking me to go out with you, Matt?' she asked, incredulous.

"In a manner of speaking, yes."

"It's a little too soon, if you ask me. Besides, I think you're just hurting."

"No, I'm not. I mean, yes, I am hurting. And no, it's not too soon." He grabbed hold of Susan's hirsute hand and held it to his cheek. "You know, I'm into BBW women."

He gave her hand a tight squeeze.

"I don't date much, Matt. Mostly because of my size. Men think it's a turn-off."

"I don't. My last girlfriend was almost three-hundred pounds."

"I guess that's a compliment, I'm not sure." Whatever else was percolating in his twisted brain, the one thing he wasn't anticipating was that Susan would lean far across the table and pucker up. Ashton closed his eyes tight, pursed his lips, and touched his to Susan's.

Not so bad, he thought. Not so bad if only he kept his eyes closed.

Half the game plan had now been accomplished. The other half was to keep Susan away from her building as much as possible. That, he realized, would take some doing. So for the next few weeks, Ashton took her on a whirlwind of outings—mostly darkened movie theatres, out-of-the-way restaurants, drives to small towns ... any place he figured he wouldn't be spotted.

He never picked her up at home, instead asking her to meet him on the street. Just his way, he explained, which Susan thought strange. "We live down the hall."

"About that," Ashton said. "I'm not there most of the time. I just pop in from time to time. Place is being renovated so there's workmen coming in and out all the time. Contractors and subs. I've rented a furnished apartment downtown."

One evening, over dinner of crab cakes, blackened catfish and dirty rice, Susan mentioned to Ashton that she saw a couple enter into his apartment. Mid-thirties, smartly-dressed. Upscale.

"I'm allowing some friends to stay over," he said, his face flushing. He hoped the heat he was feeling wasn't showing externally. "They've fallen on hard times. Down on their luck. They look normal enough but there's mental issues, you know. Just came from an addiction clinic. Both of them. It's dicey right now, touch and go." Aston breathed deeply. "Look, don't ever speak or acknowledge them, even if they say hello to you. They need their peace and quiet. They're like alabaster people—liable to fall to pieces at any time. Just look down if you see them. Right down at the ground."

"How can they live in the apartment with all the work going on?"

"The workmen are there only during the day when they're away. As for the dust, I think it's still better than a halfway house, which is where the doctors wanted to send them. I actually vouched for them. That's the only reason they were let out."

Ashton realized the web of deceit he had concocted was growing exponentially. Plus it was complicated—Parkinson's, MS, workmen, institutions, Ashton o/a Matt. He suspected Susan might ask where the couple down the hall went during the day, what their names were, how he knew them, what sort of renos were being undertaken … so many questions that his taxed brain might soon explode.

Going out with Susan was also starting to become a little taxing, for a number of reasons. First, there was the drain on his wallet. Although he told Susan he worked as an accountant, the truth was that he was unemployed and paid his rent only because of the good graces of his parents, who were very much alive and healthy. His parents, always his parents with the deep pockets, and welfare. But he never let on about his state of employment, concluding that even someone as homely as Susan might take issue with an unemployed suitor, considering that she herself had a decent job as an archivist at a museum.

There was a more pressing issue though, one Ashton wasn't sure how to resolve. Susan began pushing for something other than a platonic relationship. "It's been fifteen years since I made love with someone," she revealed to Ashton. "Since my late teens. And I think he was drunk at the time."

Not surprising, thought Ashton. He could barely stand to look at Susan. Too much hair, too many folds, pockets of skin that ended in black holes. He wondered whether he could now call off the relationship in its entirety, make a clean break. After all, he had planted the seed in Susan that she must not under any circumstance disrupt the couple living in his apartment. But he knew that could only go on for a short time—at some point soon the non-existent renovations would have to come to an end ... and if Susan were to still to see the couple ... well ...

Each Tuesday morning, Ashton continued to visit Evie's apartment. It was a great distraction from all his concerns. The apartment was quiet, tidy and neat. Just the antidote for his frazzled brain. He continued introducing items—a spool of blue thread, a bottle of B vitamins, a music CD ... it was truly wonderful fun. But soon he returned to the half-baked idea of introducing a living creature. The butterfly worked ... whatever 'worked' meant ... so why not bring in two butterflies? Which is what he did. He caught a couple in the same park as last time, although now it took him half a day. The stupid things would simply not fly in straight paths.

He rubbed his hands together in glee and watched as the Monarchs flew around Evie's apartment at bizarre angles, like crazed mini-helicoptors. As the butterflies continued to learn the nuances of their new home, Ashton decided to call it a day. Fun was fun but he had other important matters to think about, like what to do about Susan and her increasing sexual demands. He opened the window a smidge as he had the first time and left the apartment, locking the door behind him.

"Matt!"

"Susan!"

"What are you doing here?"

"Came to check up on the apartment. See how the work is going."

"I came home sick. Not feeling great. But now that I see you, I feel much better."

Ashton smiled nervously. He couldn't linger in the hallway.

"Well, I've got to run, Susan. I'll meet you for a beer tonight or tomorrow. Right after work. See ya. Gotta get back."

He tried to step around her but found his way blocked. "What about right now?" she said.

"Can't Susan. Really have to go to work."

"We won't be long. Besides, I've never been inside your place."

Before Ashton could respond, Susan had wrestled the key from his hand and was turning the lock. "Hey!" he shouted. But it was no use—she was already in the apartment and looking around.

"Nice. Very nice. Contemporary. You've got quite the eye. But where's all the work taking place?"

"Bedrooms. Both of them. Can't go in there," Ashton said, his voice quivering.

"How about that beer?"

"Beer's warm. Really warm. You don't want any of that stuff. It'll make you sick."

"My mother always gave me 7 Up if I had an upset stomach. As I grew up, I turned to warm beer, I don't know why. I think I read about it in some health magazine. And it's always worked like a charm! So warm beer will be good for my upset stomach."

With gritted teeth, Ashton searched the kitchen for a couple of warm beers.

"Lots of framed pictures of your friends," she called out. "That and ... weeeeeehhhh!!!"

"Come quick!"

Ashton bolted into the living room.

"Weeeeeehhhh! Weeeeeehhhh!" Susan continued squealing and grabbed hold of Ashton's arm. "Look! Look! Butterflies!"

"Keep it down, please," Ashton said.

"Weeeeeehhhh!"

Ashton gave her the beer he found. "Here, have a long chug. I think I'll join you."

Susan sat on the sofa, clinging to Ashton's arm and gulping her beer.

"How do you think those butterflies got in here?" she asked

"Maybe a nest outside the window. It's open a crack as you can see."

"Butterflies don't build nests, silly." She walked to the window and opened it wide.

"Shoo, shoo." In short order, the butterflies flew out.

Ashton could feel Susan's thunderous breast pushing up against his arm and the amorous look on her face made him extremely nervous. When she moved in for a kiss and bit down on his lower lip, Ashton tried to gently push her aside, but she was as immoveable as a boulder. "You're not well," he said. "And I really have to get back to work now."

Just at that moment, a look of sheer panic crossed his face. He could hear a key being inserted into the front door. He grabbed Susan's hand and ran into the bedroom.

"What's going on?"

"Sshhh," Ashton whispered, holding a finger to his lips.

He knew every corner and crevice in the apartment and his destination was a tiny five foot by five foot alcove at the rear of the closet. Ashton crept in on his hands and knees, followed by Susan.

"I didn't see any work in the bedroom."

"Sshhh." Ashton quietly closed the door to the alcove.

"What's going on?"

"Burglars," Ashton said in a low voice. "They've been here before. They're dangerous. I think it might even be the contractors themselves. Sshhh."

"It's cozy in here," Susan said, snuggling close to Ashton. "Very, very dark. Scary dark." She took a swig of beer and gave Ashton a peck on the cheek.

Ashton could hear footsteps coming closer, entering the bedroom. His heart was thumping, and his leg started twitching involuntarily.

Hangers were shuffled about in the closet and Ashton smelled Evie's perfume. He sat quietly on his haunches, staring upwards in the darkness like he was consulting higher powers.

Susan continued kissing Ashton, moving her lips from his cheek to his lips to his neck. Little nibbles that squashed his nose. His leg started twitching violently and he needed both hands to hold it still.

He could hear Evie move away from the closet. He took a shallow breath but there was little air in the alcove and it was made worse when Susan passed some gas. "Told you, bad stomach," she whispered. She took Ashton's face in her hands and kissed him hard on his lips.

Ashton slid backwards as far as he could go but Susan followed him into the corner and leaned into his limp body. He wanted to pee in the worst way. He could hear the shower turn on and realized this was his opportunity to get out.

"What sort of thieves take showers?" Susan murmured.

Saliva seeped from the corner of Ashton's mouth and he felt faint. He tried to speak but couldn't. He moved his lips again but still no sounds came out.

The entire earth, led by Susan's tremendous girth, seemed to be tilting toward the corner he was in, leaving him unable to breathe. Monarch butterflies began to emerge in the darkness. They came out in droves, a black and orange army, dotting the hillside of Ashton's beleaguered mind.

THE QUANTUM THEORY
OF LOVE AND MADNESS

I **WAS SITTING** in the church pew, listening to the pastor prattle on about the dear departed, someone I did not know, when the woman next to me began to whimper. I reached for her hand and looked at her empathically, as if to say: 'Yes, isn't it terrible about Clarisse, but at least the living can support each other.' Tears welling up in her doleful eyes, I released her hand, which I had held only lightly, and offered her a spotless white handkerchief. She dabbed at her eyes and gave my hand a squeeze. It was just the kind of reaction I had hoped for.

Funerals and wakes are the best places to meet women, I'm convinced of that. I've tried other places — hospital emergency rooms are also pretty good. The problem there is that you have to make sure the person isn't too sick. If you see someone taking greedy gulps of the stale hospital air or if blood is oozing from one of their orifices, it's probably best to stay away.

The advantage funerals or emergency rooms have over say, trying to meet someone at an art gallery opening, or

79

even online, is that in those former situations, people are undoubtedly sad or anxious, depressed even. Their guards are down and they're actually open to commiserating with others. You only need the right opening line or, in the case of Angela, the woman I met at Clarisse's funeral, a clean handkerchief.

But even funerals can be fraught with difficulties. An issue that invariably crops up is what your relationship to the deceased was. My experience in these matters has led me to conclude that it's best to let the other person talk first about how they knew the dear departed. For instance, if they were high school friends, you can go back even further than that and say you knew the dead person in elementary school. University friends are best because you have a whole history prior to that to play with.

Anyway, the secret, as I've found out, is to scan the church or synagogue for the good-looking women who are sitting by themselves. You just sidle up and take your place next to them. Now you can waste a perfectly good afternoon if the person happens to be wearing a wedding band so you have to check for that.

Following the service, I stood next to Angela at the buffet table.

"It's hard to eat during times like this," I said to her. "I don't have much of an appetite."

"Neither do I," she said, sobbing. I told her she could keep my handkerchief … women seem to like those little shows of chivalry. We went for a walk outside and Angela pulled out a cigarette.

"How did you know Clarisse?" she asked suddenly, blowing smoke rings.

I feigned some tears; I was all choked up. "I … I … " My throat constricted and I waved a beleaguered hand at her. "You go first … " I whispered.

Curiously, and it was the first time that it had ever happened to me, but the woman I was trying to pick up choked up worse that I. Angela's face turned into one contorted red mass and then it exploded into a cataclysm of tears and snot and cries. It was like the Big Bang all over again. Much to my chagrin, I had no choice but to reveal my association with the deceased first, which meant that I needed to pick my best lie.

I cleared my throat. "Well, umm … you know, we were in Grade 3 together."

Angela's face lit up and she smiled.

"You mean you went to Jesse Ketchum school?" she said in a silky voice.

My radar instinctively went up and although I could sense something was amiss, I had no way at this point to extricate myself.

"Yes, that's it. Clarisse and I—Jesse Ketchum."

Angela suddenly held a stiff arm out across my chest, stopping me dead in my tracks.

"Clarisse didn't go to Jesse Ketchum. She went to King Edward. I should know. I'm her first cousin."

I was about to embark on another lie when I could see Angela snarling at me, her eyes all scrunched up.

"You'd better come clean, mister."

I had to fess up, to reveal I was a serial woman chaser, haunting funerals and hospitals and the like. Any place where despondency prevailed, covering everyone like a shroud.

"You're a sick puppy." The words were caustic enough but curiously, the tone of Angela's voice didn't reveal disgust. Rather, it sounded contemplative, like she was planning how to turn the matter to her advantage: "Here's the deal. You're looking for a pick-up? Ok, you've found her. But I call the shots in this relationship and if you should ever do anything to annoy me or if you leave me without my consent, I'll take out a full-page ad in the newspaper telling everyone exactly what kind of person you are."

And that was how I got my new girlfriend.

Angela was no shrinking violet. She told me a story about her having gone to Japan to teach English that convinced me that I would have been taking my life in my hands had I dissed her in any way.

After a few months in Japan, Angela realized her teacher's salary wasn't going to go very far. So she got a second job at a bar called 'Rising Moon Anger Relief Bar.' She thought she was to simply have served food to Japanese businessmen, but it turned out to be more complicated than that. There was a reason why the bar was called what it was — patrons were allowed to take shots at the staff, to vent their frustrations. Angela initially wondered why most of the staff looked like sumo wrestlers, really large and obese guys. Now she knew.

On her second night at the bar, a slightly-built business type pushed her ... a good, hard shove. All of the drinks she was carrying went flying. Angela picked herself up and confronted the guy. She stood nose to nose with him and said that she now had to pay for all the spilled drinks. He just laughed so she roared back and cold-cocked him. He was out like a light and his friends had to carry him out the door.

"Anyone else?" she told the group, striking a fighter's pose.

Every night she worked there someone tried to pick a fight with her. Understandably, everyone left the sumo types alone ... so she was the fodder. She told me she became very adept at slipping or blocking punches but that sometimes the punches made their way through her defenses and actually landed. Those were the ones that set her off. She attacked with ferocious venom, pummelling the assailant. The sumos had to bodily take her off her fallen opponents. Eventually management had to let her go — they were worried about her killing someone.

After Angela told me that story, I decided I had better not do anything to upset her.

I can't deny that she was a beautiful woman. Statuesque at 5'8" with long dark hair that framed her gleaming porcelain skin and curves in all the right places, I was the envy of every guy who saw us together. But her beauty always struck me as a paradox — an outer veil concealing a hard nut inside. I learned that she had not had a boyfriend for a very long time prior to our having met. While her external beauty should have attracted men from near and far, it did not. At least, not for long. One of her close girlfriends revealed that guys did in fact flock to her but that like moths attracted to a red-hot light bulb, they got burnt and flew away quickly.

So it was no surprise that Angela wanted to hold on to me. And in truth, it wasn't all bad. Our lovemaking was terrific, we enjoyed movies, cooked up delicious dinners together, and went for long bike rides. And every once in awhile I recognized a soft spot beneath a crusty outer core —she was very kind to animals, often feeding the pigeons and squirrels in the park. She made googly eyes at children and sometimes gave change to vagrants. Once I even saw her buy a homeless guy a hot lunch and a new pair of socks.

But those moments never seemed to last. I often saw her fly into a rage at the most innocuous thing, like when I disagreed with her on whether a movie had merit or not. At those times it was like the beautiful exterior began peeling away, replaced by a heinous cackling witch—one with a long, crooked, wart-infested nose—threatening spells with her wand.

So after six months of this, I decided I needed to end it. Not only did I feel restrained, no longer able to search out women at funerals, but I became quite scared of Angela at times. Those rages.

There was a problem breaking up with Angela though. Because of the blackmail threat, I knew I couldn't leave her. My only hope was that she would leave me. So I set out to convince her to do so.

The first thing I tried was being sick. Prior to her coming over one day, I locked myself in the cold cellar of my house for two hours and drank three bottles of iced tea. When I came out and greeted her at the door, I was shivering and my lips were blue. I told Angela that I wasn't well, that I had contacted some strange disease at one of the hospital emergency rooms, one that had been dormant for years and was only now manifesting itself.

Angela wouldn't buy it. She said giving in to a foreign bug was for pansies and that she would help me fight it. She put me to bed, fitted a thick pair of woollen socks on my frozen feet, and wrapped a towel around my head. She fed me chicken soup stock for hours on end and rubbed Vick's Vapo-Rub on my chest, covering it with warm compresses. Then she made a strange concoction of herbs and spices and forced me to drink it in long gulps. I almost puked each time and begged her to stop but she would have none of it. She forced this horrible melange down my throat until I finally erupted violently in one long arc, spewing liquid and guts onto the wall. She saw that as a good sign, that all the bad stuff was finally coming out of me. Angela wouldn't leave me until I got better ... and better I did get!

Then I tried religion. I told her one day when we were cooking dinner that I felt, well ... 'different.'

"Different how?" she asked, slicing a tomato.

"Angela, as odd as this is going to sound, I think God has filled me with his love. I just feel it in every bone in my body and now he wants me to do his work. I expect I'll be going door to door with those Watchtower guys or with the Jehovah Witnesses, spreading his word."

Angela angrily stuck the tip of the knife into the cutting board so that it wobbled from side to side. Then she walked over to me and pinched me so hard on my shoulder that my eyes started to water.

"What did you do that for?" I yelled.

"I was just getting God's love out of you. The only love you're going to be filled with is a love for me! Got it?!"

I did and quickly gave up on the idea of religion as a way out.

As a last measure, I tried cross-dressing. I figured that, if she thought I was some sort of freak, she would just walk out. So I bought women's lingerie and dresses and made sure I placed them where Angela would be sure to find them. One day she did. "What is all this stuff?" she asked in a gruff manner, holding up a pair of red panties and a black leather bra.

I mooned around the apartment, fluffing it up by throwing out all the remaining women's pieces I had hidden. "Oh, you've found me out," I said in an effete way.

Much to my chagrin, Angela didn't appear angry. Quite the opposite. When she was certain that all the garments belonged to me, she asked quite demurely:

"Perhaps you can wear some of this at night, you know, when we do the dirty deed."

I had forgotten that Angela had a decided kinky side.

I thought about other possibilities. Like saying that I was running away with the circus or that I was a card-carrying member of the undead, a true-life vampire. Nothing seemed feasible.

I resigned myself to my fate and decided that, if I had to stay with this woman, I might as well make it all legit. My body shaking with dread, I got down on one knee and proposed.

Angela grabbed me by the shoulders and began shaking. "Marry you?" she yelled. "You're a skank. Why would I want to spend the rest of my life with a freak like you!

You're infested with all kinds of bacteria and parasites! If I don't catch something from you that'll cause my death, I'll go crazy with your religious proselytizing. And last but not least, I'll have to share all my clothes with you! I'm getting the hell out of your place while I still can."

I should have left it at that. Run as far away from Angela as I could, clicking my heels as I went. But I couldn't. I realized I was rootless, without any plans for the future. All of my friends were married and some had kids. I was 38 years old; to go back to prowling funerals and hospital rooms seemed untenable, just a terrible proposition. I had done it for so long and I now desperately needed some sense of permanence, someone to care for.

I didn't want to end up an old bachelor. I had often dropped by a donut shop close to where I lived where I saw first-hand the results of such a life — all these old grizzled men sitting around tables and telling stories they had told a thousand times before, some speaking Yiddish, others Polish, Russian, even English. The has-beens ate rice pudding like it was caviar, sipped on watery chicken soup, and sweetened their coffees with copious packets of white sugar. And if, heaven forbid, a woman were to enter their sanctuary, they would crawl over each like crabs making their way over the sand to the ocean, each trying to be the first to draw attention.

It was inevitable. The woman would show no interest and saunter out the door; it was then that the men would speak disparagingly of her ... *she had a big behind, her best days were long gone, did you see all the wrinkles* ... From time to time, I would notice that one of the regulars was no longer at the shop, and surmised that he must have died. Surprisingly, despite the deaths, the group seemed to grow, more and more old men joining. I didn't know where the newcomers came from, only that they must have been bachelors.

So I decided that I would not become one of the donut-shop boys. Which meant I had to give up my carousing ways and settle down. And as unlikely as it seemed, Angela appeared to be my best bet—she had some qualities I liked ... well, maybe not *liked* so much as admired: she was strong-willed, devious, and actually very, very bright ... she had me and my shenanigans figured out pretty quickly. Did I mention she was also gorgeous? And kind at times? So if she liked her sex rough or flew into a rage at the slightest provocation, maybe those were things I could get used to. Especially the sex.

So not very long after she slammed the door to my place and stomped out, telling me what a skank I was, I showed up at her door, a bouquet of red and white roses in my quivering hand.

"I'm sorry, Angela. I know I messed up big time, what with all that proselytizing and such."

"I knew you were kidding."

"You did?"

"Of course. Think I just fell off a turnip truck? I just figured you wanted me out of your life. And if someone doesn't want me around, then I don't stick around."

"Huh. You're smarter than I give you credit for."

"Excuse me?" I could see Angela's eyes narrowing and I quickly moved to hand her the flowers.

"Hey, I was just kidding, yet again." I leaned in and gave her a peck on her cheek.

"I'm afraid," she said suddenly.

"What! You afraid? I hardly think so." *Where was this going? Was she playing me?* Now that I knew, I decided to play along. "What are you afraid of anyway?"

"Many things," she said solemnly. "Dying. Growing old alone. Getting sick. If I find someone to love, I'm afraid I won't be a good partner. And if I have a kid, I'm afraid I won't be a good mom. I'm afraid of all the chaos in the world. Sometimes I'm afraid of living."

So that was it. All the cards on the table. She really wasn't kidding around. As astounded as I was, I also realized now was the time for me to make my move.

"Me too," I said. "I'm afraid of all those things. And others too."

Angela dropped the flowers and grabbed hold of my limp arms, pulling me closer. She kissed me hard on my lips and escorted me to her bedroom, where she took off all my clothes and climbed on top of me.

And that was how I got my girlfriend back again.

One Sunday morning, as we were eating a breakfast of scrambled eggs, toast and strawberry jam, Angela quite casually mentioned that she would like a child.

"What?" I nearly choked on a piece of buttered toast and spit it out.

"Oh, so gross. And you heard me."

"Are you serious?"

"I am. I mean, I'm not getting any younger. In a few years, I'll turn 40 and then having a kid becomes harder, and more dangerous. It's now or never, really."

"I thought you said you were afraid you might not be a good mom."

"I did say that. I did. And I was being truthful. I'll just try and overcome it, that's all."

"Ok, I'm afraid too." And this time, I really did mean it.

"Let's go for it," Angela said, kissing me on my forehead. "Together."

"I think I always wanted a baby," I said softly. The words slipped out, like someone had clapped me on the back and expelled them.

And then the oddest thing happened—I could see Angela dissolving, the mean, ugly, shrewish part of her that is, leaving only her angelic side. Sitting there in her white nightgown, her hair shimmering from the ceiling lights, she was quite the sight—dazzling, beautiful, and whole. Happy. I could have sworn I saw an angel trumpeting above her shoulder, and the moonlight now replacing the kitchen lights. Stars too. It was me of course, just me and my imagination. But still, I guess I really did want to be a father. Maybe I never really wanted to be a shiftless skank—I could do better. And together, just like she said, maybe we could overcome our fears.

Angela hugged me and her face lit up. "I didn't know what you would say," she said.

"Now you know."

"Just one more thing."

"Ok"

"I'm already pregnant."

Shortly after that eventful breakfast, I started to put my head close to Angela's belly and sing. I had heard that babies bonded with their parents that way. Even Angela thought it was a good idea. The trouble was that I didn't know many songs—the only two I knew were Eminem rap songs.

"Maybe not so good," Angela said. "Don't you know anything else? Like Beatle songs?"

"I grew up with Eminem, what can I say."

"Try talking some science then. Even math. I've read that if you teach an unborn addition and subtraction, you might end up with a very bright baby."

I was terrible at math, and science wasn't my thing either. I was just an ordinary Joe, a college drop-out, with a job as an assistant manager at a second-run movie theatre; in my spare time, I liked to bet on the ponies at the race-track. So what did I know about such things as math and science?

But now, after Angela asked me to talk some science, something changed in me—I suddenly became quite interested in the subject. The very thing I once despised in high school. I didn't want to let Angela down. But there was something else: Now that I was about to be a father, I wanted to have a greater understanding of life. Eggs and sperm and babies and all that.

It was all very strange, something I had never thought about before. I mean, how could my DNA mix with some-one else's DNA and create life? Is that what happened? I might have understood if I had known exactly what DNA was. But I didn't even know that. I asked a few friends down at the racetrack, but nobody had a clue. Someone thought it was the name of a filly.

I had to read on my own. Which meant that I borrowed books from the library, science stuff, baby stuff. I also spent hours googling websites. Interestingly, the more I read, the more I wanted to read. The more answers I got, the more answers I wanted. And because there was so much to know, and I knew so little, I felt as though there was a black hole in my mind. A total void that I had to fill up. So in addition to baby books and a bit of chemistry, I started reading about physics. And it all created this incredible rush of adrenaline, a hunger to keep on learning.

I soldiered on, for Angela, and for the little one who was yet to be born. And it was filling up that void in me and made me feel, well ... kind of happy, fulfilled, as odd as that appeared. And it made me believe, maybe for the very first time in my life, that I wasn't as dumb as all that, that I could actually learn things if only I applied myself.

I was drawn to Quantum Theory. Imagine! Quantum Physics. Particularly that. It talked about waves and atoms and electrons and reduced everything in the universe down to the smallest particles, stating that energy can be absorbed or emitted by matter only in these very tiny microscopic particles that the German physicist Max Plank called *Quanta*. And furthermore, that these atoms and their constituents exhibited dual-like behaviour, specifically both wave-like and particle-like behaviour. So what if they showed this duality, why was that interesting? To be honest, I didn't even truly understand what *particle behaviour* and *wave-like behaviour* meant. It was all too obtuse. But I read on ... and on ... and started to pick things up, if even on a superficial level, and found myself embroiled in the midst of the great mysteries of life.

I read about another German physicist—Werner Heisenberg. He seemed to take Plank's Quantum Theory even further, at least that's how I saw it, saying that certain pairs of variables associated with these microscopic particles, cannot both be known. So for instance, if the speed of a sub-atomic particle—that being one variable—is known, then the other variable, the location, cannot be known. And vice-versa. He called it the *Uncertainty Principle*.

So what did it all mean? And why was I drawn to it, this Uncertainty Principle? I only had vague ideas, it was baffling, all this murkiness at the sub-atomic level. So I formed my own theory, using the little knowledge I was able to understand. And that was: that my baby was starting out as a small mass of electrons, neutrons and protons, absorbing energy from the food Angela was providing her, and growing. No big revelation there because for sure she was growing, I could see it as my girlfriend's stomach grew larger and larger. Emitting too! Emitting energy, kicking, as Angela would tell me.

But the uncertainty of where those particles were at any one time, the speed at which they moved, all that, now made perfect sense, at least to me. It was my own theory, I guess, attributing well-known physics theories to people. But it explained why Angela was so volatile; if her energy was emitted by the smallest particles ever and they were here, there, everywhere, beyond our knowing, then it struck me that anyone's personality wasn't a certainty, that it was readily changeable at any time. After all, since we were made of these infinitely minute particles; it had to be

then that like flotsam in the sea, our essences, our personalities, were constantly adrift; anything could move them
... like the waves of the ocean. Like the waves of atoms.

Wow, I was getting it. Or maybe not, I didn't know. But
what I realized was that, like those microscopic particles,
everything in life was random. So much happened just by
chance. You couldn't predict anything. You could cross the
street one day, on your way to the donut shop, and get killed
by a car. Ok, so I wasn't about to revolutionize physics.
Nor win a Nobel Prize. But all this reading allowed me to
appreciate Angela's uncertainty, mine too for that matter.
Everyone's really. Our madness, our volatility. Also that because of that uncertainty, I could change, I was changing.
I stopped going to the racetrack. I was too busy talking to
our baby. Talking chemistry, physics, and some math.

Embrace the uncertainty, that became my motto. Because along with that came possibilities. And when our
baby was born, Emma was her name, all possibilities came
to life. I realized something else then. That I loved her so
much that it hurt, I actually ached when I saw her for the
first time in the delivery room. I loved Emma down to her
last electron, her last quanta, her last atom. Every sub-atomic particle. Every last one. Ah yes, the quantum theory of
madness, and now of love ... it was all so unpredictable,
but there was nothing quite like it. I never knew random-
ness could feel so good.

STARCHILD

MY EARLIEST RECOLLECTION of the "disorder" was when I was about six, perhaps seven. It was at that time that my mother took me to a doctor. "He just babbles," she said. "Early on he used to talk. But now, no words. He's regressed and we don't know why."

The doctor examined me and concluded that all of the tools were in place—pharynx, larynx, vocal cords. "He should be speaking in full sentences," he said. "It's a mystery right now." He removed the tongue depressor and made me repeat certain sounds after him—"ooohh, aaahh, baaa." Although I understood what he wanted, I wouldn't utter a single note. Only when he shrugged his shoulders and told me I was free to go did I decide to help him out. I reached deep into my gut and sang out: "*I feel good.*"

My mother threw her hands up in the air like she was signalling a football touchdown and my sister, who had accompanied us, alternated between hugging and kissing me. Even the man in the white coat with the stethoscope around his neck broke into a big smile: "Sing that again," he asked. So I did.

The doctor looked at my mother. "Isn't that from a James Brown song? I love music and that sounds a lot like it."

"Well, we do listen to a lot of music around the house," she said. "So maybe he just picked it up. Anyway, I think you're right ... it does sound a lot like James Brown."

The doctor addressed me directly: "Can you just *say* those words—*I feel good*—and not sing them?"

Maybe I could. But I wouldn't do it. No way. I just kept my mouth shut.

That was the beginning. From that time on, I sang everything, the words all coming from songs I knew. Although everyone concluded that my new-found mode of communication was a lot better than my not saying anything, it really didn't improve my overall situation. In fact, it made it worse. Now that it was determined that I could in fact talk, everyone wanted more of me. They wanted me to talk, just like other kids. Like adults. So I was sent to a new set of doctors—child psychiatrists.

The head doctors weren't very sympathetic. They pressed me over and over again as to why I wouldn't talk in the 'normal manner.' What are you hiding? What are you covering up? What are you compensating for? They brutalized me but I wouldn't give in ... I just shook my head and wouldn't say a word. Actually, it was quite easy to fool them —they concluded that I was a very sensitive child, some sort of highly unusual savant. One told my mother as much. "His condition isn't even listed in the DSM-5," he said. "It's like the psychiatric bible—every known condition is listed ... but not this one. Your son is one-of-a-kind."

So, if the doctors wanted to think as much, that was fine — it kept my own secret safe.

Of course James Brown wasn't the only singer whose words I sang. But they were the first. My mother was right, music was played all the time in our house, so I was able to pick up a lot. A lot. There were lyrics to show anger or jealousy, to express sadness and happiness, to say I was hungry or ill or lonely, to reveal all of my wants and desires ... the list was endless.

By the time I was nine, I had learned the words to over six hundred songs and the doctors now had a label they could attach to me — *Lyric Savant*. Someone who can't speak in normal language but is so gifted and disordered that he can learn hundreds upon hundreds of songs by rote.

"We will try to get this psychiatric condition listed in the DSM-6, whenever it comes out," said that same doctor who had previously told my mother about the DSM-5. "It'll be a first."

Now that my problem had been diagnosed, efforts were made to remedy the situation. The psychiatrists sent me to speech pathologists. For the most part, they attempted to slow down the cadence of the songs to the point that I was literally talking, not singing. They stretched words out into individual syllables and took them down a notch further, literally mouthing the sounds for me: Y-O-O-O-O-U-D-E-E-S-E-R-R-V-E-A-A-A-B-R-E-E-A-A-K-T-O-O-O-D-A-Y.

I knew what they were up to. Plus I didn't appreciate them butchering songs or in this case, a McDonald's jingle. I liked the food at McDonald's. The place was kid friendly. So I just sang the jingle the way I normally sang everything, ignoring the slow motion versions.

On one occasion, a very clever speech pathologist played me a song by Leonard Cohen entitled *Everybody Knows*. He asked that I sing along. As a rule, I tried to stay away from Cohen's repertoire. He didn't sing his songs as much as walk through them. The same way Bob Dylan did. If Chuck Berry or the Rolling Stones were hares, Cohen was the tortoise.

As the words I knew well filtered through to me, I shrugged my shoulders and remained mute. Cajoled further by the therapist, I cupped my hands over my face and tears cascaded down. When my mother saw what was happening, she put an abrupt end to the proceedings. "Leonard Cohen has that effect on my son, I'm afraid," she said. "I can't figure it out."

"Well, if you ask me, Cohen's a bit gloomy," the therapist said. "So maybe that's it. Who knows."

Who did know? Well, I did. For instance, I knew that I was no savant. Sure I knew a lot of songs but it was necessary. I mean, in order to carry on a conversation, I needed many, many phrases. I could have talked—that would have made my life a lot easier. But I didn't want to make my life easier, I wanted to make it different. If I had spoken in the normal manner, I would have been like everyone else. And nobody, not anyone I knew anyway, was like me.

At the school I go, there are many kids who don't fit into society's norms. Richard Hayman is about my age, fourteen or so. He's tall and gangly with red hair that is as thick as an orang-utan's. As far as I'm concerned, he's really weird. They say he's a *Synesthete,* which means that he can see the alphabet in colour and experience touch and tastes that same way. Apparently he can even see colours when he hears music. I don't know about all that; when I sing to him, he never mentions blue or red or purple. Not even grey. Maybe he just wants attention.

There are other students in the school who are genuinely special. There's Diane Bell, who is awesome with numbers. Give here a six digit number to multiply by a seven digit number and she'll give you the answer in no time at all. Her nickname is the *Human Calculator.* Joseph Galbraith can play Bach's Sonatas for violin and keyboard. He's fifteen so you might think that that's no big deal but when I tell you he's been able to do that since he was four, you'll change your mind. No one knows how he could have played such complicated pieces at such a young age. He's really something. Give him any classical instrument and he'll play it perfectly—violin, keyboard, chamber organ, cello, harpsichord. No lessons, imagine.

Lars Bjornson is my best friend at school. He's a hardcore science guy, able to understand things like string theory and black holes and the double helix nature of DNA. He's got a good mind, extraordinary really. I like it when he goes to the blackboard to correct the teacher during our physics class, marking it up with all sorts of long equations. His scientific mind is as good as there is here; it could almost create a chasm into a black hole and bring in some light. But it can't. It's firmly rooted on the earth and in some ways, his calculations are simplistic. Of course I never tell him—that would ruin our friendship.

All of the classes have been designed for us special

kids. Physics, astronomy, math, music, anatomy, biochemistry, languages, engineering, law, literature ... the list is quite endless. We get to choose whatever strikes our fancy. My favourite is religion class. I didn't know much about the bible before but I've found out that people like Enoch and Elijah just disappeared from the earth. Vanished. I think what happened is that they were taken to other planets. There's no proof of course but that's my best guess. I've read that some people say they were mentally unstable and just found a hiding place, far removed from the people they knew. I read that but I don't believe it, it sounds like hooey to me.

There's lots of talent at the school but no one is like me. No one communicates solely by singing. Even amongst all the special kids, I'm unique. But this is my last year there and I'm not sure where I'll go after. It frightens me to think about what'll happen once school is over. Only there do people allow me to be myself. There and with my mother. Everywhere else it's conform or else.

Away from school, it's sometimes easier to be mute. Stay in my room and not sing a word. Just read. It's where I find peace, where I don't have to pretend. One of my favourite classes is called *Literal and Metaphorical Insights into the Novel;* there's always something wonderful to read as part of our assignments. Dostoevsky, D.H. Lawrence, Jane Austen. Great novelists all, but my favourite, my all-time favourite, is Arthur C. Clarke, the science fiction writer. *2001: A Space Odyssey, The Sands of Mars, Childhood's End*—all flights of fancy that take me away into other realms. Far, far away from the earthly plane.

Down the back steps and into the pouring rain I stood one fall afternoon, an umbrella in one hand. I could see my mother through the kitchen window, watching and wondering. She opened the door a crack and was joined by my sister. I sang out that I was waiting for a Starman.

"That's from a David Bowie song," I heard her tell my mother. She took a bite of her sandwich and said: "I like so can't believe I'm related to him. He's insane."

Insane? I narrowed my eyes and my sister moved away from the door.

How to tell my mother that I am waiting in the backyard for the mothership to come and collect their son? That she has only raised me for others? She is close to me, protects me, and has done a wonderful job raising me. With all my heart, I love her. Right now though, it is best to simply give her little hints. In time, when I feel she's ready, I'll reveal all the details. She won't like it, will be so upset, but sometimes the truth hurts.

The mothership knows all. I know a lot, but it knows more. I can't deny that. Like, where exactly my roots emanate from, I am not certain. It knows, not me. I only know that my origin is from elsewhere. Light years away. I also know that the bump I have on my back is an otherworld implant meant to keep track of me, despite my mother's insistence that it is a benign cyst. She took me to a doctor, who told her that, but we know all about doctors ... how much they know and especially how much they don't.

I have not spoken of my earth father but there is little to say. He is a drunk and walks around the house like a demented person, touching and grabbing me. He has been that way since I was very tiny. Often he reaches for my hand and pretends to be a palm reader: "Let me see," he burbles. "This here is a real deep line. It means that in the future I will fly with you to the stars." Then he laughs loudly and flashes me a smile full of worn teeth. I can smell the stink from his mouth. The funny thing is that, although I detest him and have always been afraid of him, he is right about the stars. What he doesn't know though is that only one of us will be taking that trip.

Because there are so many special kids at school, companies looking for unusual talent often come around, offering jobs. So one day, my mother accompanied me to school and approached the principal: "Can you keep an eye out for my son?" she said. "That would be greatly appreciated. He can use the work, get some real job experience, but to tell you the truth, he's a bit, well … different. You know that. And he's fragile. He can't talk like others but he is wonderful with his hands though."

Fragile, huh? I didn't say anything but that rankled. One day I would show her who was fragile indeed. Not me. Not me.

Not long after that meeting, the principal told my mother about a job opening with the *Lego Company*. So I went to their factory for some testing and kept my mouth shut throughout, letting my mother do all the talking. They gave me a bucket of two thousand Lego blocks and allowed me forty-five minutes to build an animal. Build an animal?! It was almost an insult; it took me seven minutes —I built a pink cat riding on a blue reindeer. Then they wanted me to erect two connecting spheres using square blocks. It was too easy: I built the spheres within a hexagon and I could see the Lego representatives sitting nearby, shaking their heads in awe.

Now that school is over, I spend most of my time working for Lego. It's perfect because I can do the job from my room. For the most part, I'm relaxed there. If I hear my earth father coming close, yelling stupid things, I just stop and hold my breath until he leaves. He's dumb and I don't need the interruptions. And so when I finish a model, the company has a courier pick it up. Most of what I make is intended for hobby shows and department store window displays.

Once I was told to construct a store window display for Christmas. It was a small city, complete with running railroad, a twirling windmill, different buildings—a police station, bakery, hospital, bus terminal, school. Because the construction was intricate and delicate and quite large, I had to work right in the store window. It was just impossible to transport it from my room.

At first I remained behind a closed curtain, but later removed it. It was good to see the people gathered on the sidewalk, looking in. I smiled and children waved, their eyes bright. Even though we were separated by a thick pane of glass, it was a nice feeling, being somewhat connected. Since I left school, I have had little contact with anyone. Lars moved on to university in another city, so I never see him. Actually, I don't really have any friends. Just my earth mother, I guess. Not even my sister is interested, especially of late. She is hardly ever at home and my earth mother says she has become promiscuous, whatever that means.

I am sinking in a cold, muddy wasteland. I can hear my sister call out in a panic to my mother: "Ma, you'd better come. He's standing in the backyard again, this time without any shoes or socks."

When I raised my eyes to the sky, I saw a light so bright it nearly blinded me. I stood rooted to the spot but it wasn't the sign I had been waiting for. It was a shooting star or some such anomaly. I did not despair; it was disappointing to be certain but I know the real item is forthcoming. These things take time—they are coming from afar, light years,—and I must be patient.

Patience. It is something earthlings have little of. I am continually harassed by the doctors, who demand that I speak in a normal manner. They have never left me alone, not ever. They just want me to be like everyone else. They have always insisted on it and as I have gotten older, they have become more relentless, telling my mother that it's a psychological thing with me, that I had better outgrow it otherwise I will have a very hard life as an adult. A very hard life indeed.

And as the years have passed and I have now been relegated to a life building things with blocks within the confines of my bedroom, not to mention my frequent forays standing looking at the skies in the backyard, she has relented. My own earth mother has forsaken me, given in to the snake-oil salesmen, who masquerade as doctors. She does what they say, crying that she has no choice.

"Why are you protecting him?" they badger her. I have heard those words.

"Nothing. Nothing. I'm hiding nothing from you. I'm not protecting him."

Even though I hate that she does not have more will-power, in a strange way, I understand the whole business of not having a choice.

So as the doctors finally get their way, the drugs they infuse me with seep deep into my arm. It will only make him better, they tell me mother, who repeats their words verbatim to me: It will only make you feel better, son. Sleep, she says, kissing my forehead. It's for the best. Then she closes the lights and leaves me all alone. Like I haven't been alone enough.

When I get home from the hospital, the aliens are waiting for me. Right in my bedroom. I view them slightly askew, through a mist of cloudy tears. The drugs, perhaps. Or maybe just because I am so very happy to finally see them, my people. Straight from the mothership. No, upon a moment of reflection, maybe not so happy after all. Maybe not at all.

Actually, I can barely see, it is like looking through a thick veil, but it doesn't really matter anyway—I can literally sense their presence. It's an instinctual thing. I take the bat my earth father often used on my earth mother and on my sister and marched them through the kitchen and into the backyard, right back to their ship. They were scared as I wielded it high in the air, and they had every right to be so ... that bat was very, very hard. Rock hard. I remember when my wretched earth father hit me with it, once, twice, maybe more than that ... right between the shoulder blades and on my arms.

"You abandoned me," I say slowly and clearly. "And it caused me a lot of anguish. A lot." I don't have to sing because I'm amongst my own kind. At long last.

"Don't be so hasty," the leader, my true father, says. "Your being here allowed you to grow and experience new things." He touches my arm tenderly with his crooked, reed-like fingers. "We're off to another galaxy. There's beryllium to harvest. It's not very far so we should be back in no time. Perhaps by then you'll have settled down and we can talk about leaving. Be patient." Then they disappear. Just vanish.

I return to my room, the hollow word *patient* ringing in my ears, and wipe the wetness from my eyes. I realize now that these are tears of helplessness, leading to an unremitting truth: I might have to remain on this planet for a very long time.

I play with my Lego blocks. Since I have been away for a time, I am behind on my assignments. I begin to construct a dinosaur, a Tyrannosaurus Rex. It is easy, or should be, but is not; I put blocks on backwards and upside down and the vision of models that I could always formulate with ease in my mind has vanished.

DATING AT YOUR PERIL

HIS HEAD TILTED at an angle, Cecil glanced at his image and let out a groan. A remnant from his dinner—a bubble of peanut butter—adorned his upper lip, firmly ensconced within the hairs of his moustache. He placed his forehead onto the glass pane of the jewellery store on Bloor Street and with his fingernail, began to scratch away at the intrusion. When he realized that the task was more difficult than he imagined—the peanut butter seemed to migrate the more he wiped at it—a wave of panic started to overtake him. Already he was looking less than whom he had represented himself, more like his real self. He breathed deeply and continued on, using the window of the store as his mirror.

Cecil lifted the bottom of the worn black sweatshirt he was wearing and like a Buddha proffering an abundance of good luck, rubbed his ample gut. But when he put his forehead onto the pane and closed his eyes, he let out a sigh ... his luck seemed to be running out. *Just a middle-aged boomer looking for companionship,* he thought. *Cecil Rosenblatt—spreader of good cheer, that's me.* He repeated the words *spreader of good cheer* over and over, like a mantra.

He thought about all the lies ... no, the slight mis-representations he had told her. Everyone did that on these dating sites, he told himself. Still in all, he wasn't 5'10" ... more like 5'8". And not exactly in shape ... no, not at all. But worst is that he was only a law clerk ... not a lawyer. Was that the worst?

Cecil looked at his watch. 10:40 pm. Now he was ten minutes late and still the peanut butter remained. He bought a bottle of water from a variety store and used it to wash his moustache. For good measure he also washed down the rest of his goatee, just in case.

He pulled up his baggy jeans and ran up Bloor. At Yonge Street, Starbucks came into view and Cecil stopped to collect himself. He could see a woman standing in front —it had to be her.

Cecil languidly wiped at his still-wet beard. Water dotted his sweatshirt. Maybe this was all wrong. They had forged a pretty nice correspondence via e-mail and even spoken on the phone a handful of times. Why ruin something so good? How could it possibly get any better?

At 8:30 that same evening, Elizabeth Cohen put on a Celia Cruz CD and danced around her living room. For the past year, she had taken salsa dancing lessons and loved it.

"Can I have this dance?" Elizabeth held out her hand and danced with an imaginary partner. Dancing made her feel alive again. After her marriage of ten years fell apart, she needed something to make her forget and move on.

Excited about meeting Cecil, she felt as happy as she had in a long time. They had exchanged photographs so she knew he wasn't exactly a walk down Hollywood—he was overweight and balding—but Elizabeth didn't care. At forty-six, she now knew what mattered—kindness, humour, empathy. For three months she had fostered a wonderful relationship with a funny, caring man. Sophisticated too ... he liked classical music, even foreign films. A real *mensch,* he volunteered at a local dog shelter. And he was a lawyer to boot! Not to mention that he was Jewish, an added bonus. It was all good. So very good. Now they would meet and it couldn't come any sooner for her.

10:30 at night seemed like a strange time to meet but that's what Cecil wanted. "I look better in low-light conditions," he told her. She loved his off-the-wall humour. But actually, she knew Monday night was football night—Monday Night Football—and that Cecil was a big fan. Although she herself had no interest in the sport, it was alright; people didn't have to have the exact same interests —there were more important things. Cecil wasn't interested in dancing. So 10:30 was just fine.

Elizabeth danced into her bedroom and threw off her wool bathrobe. *Nothing to wear,* she thought as she thumbed through her closet. She tried on a number of blouses but none seemed to match the brown suede skirt she had bought for the occasion. She finally settled on her reliable white silk blouse, accenting it with a black vest.

At 9:15 she took out the apricot noodle kugel from the

oven. Kugel was a favourite of Cecil's, so he had told her, and she thought she'd surprise him.

At 9:30 she took her dog Cujo out for his evening walk around Withrow Park. "Late night," she told him. "You'll have to go to sleep without me." Back in her apartment, she checked her image in the mirror one last time and sprayed herself with a hint of perfume. Then she left to meet Cecil.

She kissed him lightly on both cheeks.

"Sorry I'm late," he said, breathless.

"No worries. But your beard. It's all wet."

"You know, I was trying to get the peanut butter out."

Elizabeth flashed Cecil a big grin. "I'm sure there's a joke in there somewhere that I don't quite get. But I love your sense of humour."

Cecil said nothing. A flash of anxiety constricted his chest. *How stupid could he be?*

Elizabeth brought forth the kugel from a plastic bag. "Thought you'd enjoy this."

Cecil stared at the kugel for a long time. "You didn't have to," he said without looking up. "But thank you. Thank you very much."

The couple walked down Yonge Street with no particular destination. Elizabeth snuck glances at her companion and finally took Cecil's arm. "When I was young, my sister and I used to make up names for the constellations." She pointed skyward. "See up there? We called that one 'Jimmy Durante's Nose'."

"It sort of looks like his big schnoz," Cecil said. "I can see the resemblance."

With each step Cecil took, his arm intertwined with Elizabeth's, he became aware of his inadequacies. Right foot forward—nearly bald. Left foot forward—twenty-five pounds overweight. Right foot again—creaky, crackity knees ... click, clack ... Left foot now—alone, no partner for a very, very long time. Right—schlemiel. Left, right, left, right.

Elizabeth, a couple of inches taller, took long strides and Cecil's chunky legs hurried to keep up. "I saw a cartoon in *The Sun* today," he said. "Want to hear it?"

"Sure."

"Two Dalmatians are sitting at a computer looking at a dating site when one says to the other: 'Know what I like about the internet dating? When you send e-mails to someone, nobody knows you're a dog.'"

Elizabeth stopped abruptly and untangled her arm from Cecil's. "Cecil, are you trying to tell me something?" Her voice was tense.

Cecil lifted both hands in the air, as if he were being held up at gunpoint.

"Just a joke," he said, stammering. "Just a joke."

At Allen's Restaurant on the Danforth, they shared a plate of sweet potato French fries and a litre of red wine.

"You know, I have a lot of trepidation about meeting people on-line," Elizabeth said. "I always try to keep my expectations low. That way, you never get hurt. I try, but I'm not always successful. But then I met you and we've developed something special, I believe. Three months of corresponding and I think you get to know someone. In my opinion, friendship is the best foundation for something longer-term. How do you feel about that?"

Cecil fingered his beard. *Great body,* he thought dreamily, looking at Elizabeth. *Great face. Sharp dresser. Smart. Can't do better than this.*

"Listen, I totally agree," he said. "I'm very slow off the mark when it comes to relationships. I need to be friends first. In my books, intimacy can't be achieved without getting to know someone on a deep, deep level."

"That's exactly how I feel. Exactly."

Their forks speared the same fry and they laughed heartily, lifting it high in the air.

"Make a wish," Elizabeth said. "Then let's pull it apart."

"Like a turkey wishbone."

"Right."

Cecil closed his eyes for a second. "Now," he said.

When the fry was broken, Cecil saw that he had the larger portion. *Maybe my luck is changing after all,* he thought.

"So tell me about your job," Elizabeth said.

"What would you like to know?"

"I don't know. What's it like to be a criminal lawyer anyway?"

"Well, you know that I end up defending a lot of bad people," Cecil said, without missing a beat. "But somebody has to. I just look upon my clients as people who have made bad decisions, that's all. I believe most are good at heart."

"Very magnanimous attitude."

"What's ... oops."

"What's *what*?"

"No, nothing," Cecil said, touching his hand to his forehead, like he was chastising himself. "I always do that, change the subject. So stupid of me. I was just going to ask you about your family but then I realized we were still talking about my job."

"It's ok," Elizabeth said. "Quick mind, that's what I call it. Anyway, I can tell you about my family."

So she did. And when she was through, she asked Cecil about his.

"Well my mother died a few years ago," he said. "I was very close to her and, to tell you the truth, I really miss her."

"I like that very much in a man, Mr. Rosenblatt. Someone who's not afraid to reveal his true feelings."

The evening passed quickly, Cecil revealing his favourite foreign films, his love of Jewish cooking, even his volunteer work at the dog shelter. "I put in two hours every week, just walking the dogs. They need the companionship and also the exercise. I really look forward to it."

"Boy, you must be busy then. I mean, working full-time and also volunteering."

"Yeah, yeah, I am. But it's my way of giving back ... volunteering, that is."

"I don't think I could do it. I'd become too attached to the animals and want to take them all home."

"There's that. But it's like the criminals I represent—I

just try and distance myself so it becomes a job. They both become jobs in the end."

Elizabeth gazed at Cecil and said nothing, smiling. Cecil reciprocated as best he could but found himself uncomfortable locking eyes. He pulled on his goatee. "All dry now," he said.

Elizabeth touched it. "Yup, all dry now."

Cecil stood up abruptly. "Would you excuse me, Liz," he said. "Nature calls."

In the washroom, Cecil splashed cold water on his face and took a deep breath. Then another. Oh, where had he gone wrong? *Magnanimous* … what the hell did that mean? And *criminal lawyer? Volunteer at a dog shelter?* He could have bashed his head against the wall. Maybe he should have said he was a pornographer, whatever that entailed. He certainly had some experience with the matter. Or a retired NFL football player. Well maybe a former university player, that would have been more believable. He had watched enough football games to talk it up, no problem. But those other things. *Why, oh why?*

Cecil decided he would have to do it right from here on in. Face up to things. He walked with determination back to the table and placed both hands at either end, ready to make his point.

"Liz," he said in a steady voice. "There's something I have to tell you."

"Of course, Cecil. Whatever."

"Well, the thing is. You're not my type. I'm really sorry."

And with those words, Cecil picked up the kugel and headed to the door. Outside, buoyed by a surge of giddiness, he jumped up twice, clicking his heels each time, as if he were ridding the bottom of his shoes of some gunk. "Oy, can she talk," he said to himself.

As he continued on home, Cecil felt a great weight lift from his shoulders. He would never talk to the woman again, but that was okay ... it was a learning experience. And next time would be better. There would always be a *next time*. There were a million women online, a virtual candy store. And as he thought about it further, he was grateful that he would never have to actually *watch* a foreign film, reading about them so he could impress was awful enough. Ingmar Bergman and Jean Renoir ... slow and **boring**. Just dreadful.

Suddenly he became aware that he was being followed. He turned, but not quickly enough. A chill went through his body as someone's fist buried itself in his spongy stomach. He dropped to his knees.

"Gimme what you have," the punk said, his oily hair matted close to his forehead.

Cecil blanched and sweat trickled down his face. He tried to inhale but could only manage a mottled wheeze.

"Hand over the plastic bag. NOW!"

Cecil did as he was told.

"Noodle bread?!" the assailant said, a glazed look in his eyes. "Freakin' noodle bread?"

The punk removed the wallet from Cecil's pocket. "At least this is something," he said, before sprinting away.

"Help! Police! Police!"

As Elizabeth came running, she suddenly gasped in surprise; the very last thing she expected was to find her date for the evening lying on the ground. She was soon surrounded by a battalion of well-meaning passers-by.

"Liz, I didn't mean ..." The words slithered out the corner of Cecil's open mouth.

"Don't try and talk," she replied, trying to remain calm. She bent down low onto her haunches and held Cecil's hand. "You'll be fine. Just fine."

At Mount Sinai Hospital on University Avenue, Cecil complained bitterly about small anxious tremors. "I almost died," he told one of the nurses. At his insistence, he stayed on overnight.

Elizabeth visited the next day, bringing cheese blintzes and liver knishes.

"You shouldn't have," Cecil whispered.

"No bother at all. People should be there for others during times of need."

"I haven't seen this much good Jewish food since my mother died. You know, at the shiva."

"I guess you don't cook much for yourself."

"No, mostly I eat peanut butter and bagels. You can't go wrong with bagels. I get mine at a store on Eglinton. But, you know, sardines are good too."

"Well, enjoy."

Cecil grinned. "Hey Liz, I got hit pretty hard. Have a look." He lifted his nightshirt.

Elizabeth could only see a very faint purple mark just below Cecil's ribcage.

"Bad, huh?"

"Well, doesn't look too too bad."

"Oh, it's bad all right. A heart punch, that's what the

coward gave me. I know because I've seen it done in wrestling. Right smack over the heart. People die from those kinds of punches, you know."

Cecil reflected for a moment and continued: "But the good thing is that you saved my life, calling the paramedics and all."

"Well, t'was nothing. Just wait till you get my bill though."

Cecil stifled a laugh. "Oh, hurts." He exhaled and closed his eyes. "But how did you know where I was anyway?"

"Call it serendipity. I happened to live close by, just off Pape Avenue, and was on my way home. I actually had no idea it was you until I got close up. I just saw the guy standing over someone and screamed until he ran."

"My lucky day."

"What was he after anyway?"

"Money, I guess. He took your kugel."

"Wow, I knew my kugel was popular. I just didn't know it was **that** popular!"

Cecil laughed this time, holding his stomach. "Look Liz," he said. "There's something I want to tell you."

"Again?" she deadpanned.

"Again."

"Ok. Go for it."

"Well, it's this. I didn't mean what I said in the restaurant. I was just ... well, just scared. I have all these insecurities and didn't think I was good enough for you. But the fact of the matter is that you're a great woman. Like another mother to me. I know it's a long shot now but I'd really like to get to know you better. We can be great together, I'm sure of it. Just need some time, that's all."

Elizabeth sighed. "I have to tell you, Cecil. You're different from what I imagined. I mean, I don't know what to believe now, it's confusing. And maybe even it's my fault; investing too much in someone I don't really know. But, I don't think so. Like, last night when I got home, I just thought I would google your law firm. Just to have a look through the roster of lawyers … you weren't even listed."

"Ah, that." Cecil held up a forefinger, determined to set the matter straight, like the defense lawyer he wasn't. "I just started there pretty recently, Liz. So they haven't had the time to put up a pic of me. It's pretty simple."

Elizabeth shook her head. "Anyway, I guess the point is that whatever it was that was open when we first met has since closed up for me. I have to go with my gut, and it's telling me 'no.' You're a nice guy but maybe not what I'm looking for. Sorry."

And with those words, Elizabeth departed the hospital. It was a warm, clear evening, and she decided to walk up University Avenue, then east on Bloor Street and along the Bloor Street Viaduct. She ran her hands along the wire suicide barrier and stared down into the Don Valley Parkway. Every time she walked along the bridge, she thought of the many singers who had sung about it—Bruce Cockburn, The Spoons … ah yes, The Spoons' *Romantic Traffic*. What a great song.

On the Danforth, she stopped at the Big Carrot for a quick meal of lentil soup, cheese quiche, and garden salad. Returning home, she was greeted enthusiastically by Cujo, who jumped and jumped. She lifted him tight to her chest and floated around the room, seemingly in time to an imaginary waltz. But feeling distracted, she stopped abruptly.

With eyes glistening, she changed into pyjamas and made herself a cup of mint tea. She considered going on-line, to the dating site she had frequented when she met Cecil, but instead slipped into bed and picked up one of the books she kept on her bedside table—*The Tevye Stories*. It was given to her as a gift by her mother after the two had gone to see a Broadway production of *Fiddler on the Roof.* She read the inside sleeve:

> *These delightful tales of Tevye the Milkman formed the basis for the musical "Fiddler on the Roof." They tell the story of ruin, some of which can be traced back to the antics of the main character himself. Tevye is at once foolish, exasperating, warm, kind, earthy and funny. He sees himself through his hard times by recalling Talmudic or biblical quotations, usually rather garbled and incomprehensible. Above all else, Tevye remains the indestructible optimist with a spirit that refuses to be crushed. Laced with his commonsense view of life, the classic stories of Tevye will charm the modern reader.*

Elizabeth picked a story—*Tevye Loses a Small Fortune*—and began reading. A slight smile occasionally curling her lips, she read for about twenty minutes, With her eyelids closing on her, she turned off the night lamp and fell into blissful sleep.

THE DOCTOR IS IN

BESET WITH INSOMNIA, I rose from bed and ambled to the kitchen. The grapes, I knew, were on the table and as I lifted the bunch and stuffed a handful into my cavernous mouth, a solitary one dropped onto the floor. It brushed against my foot and rolled away. I returned to bed but the thought of the wayward berry gnawed at my brain. I tiptoed ever so quietly back into the kitchen, as if by doing so, I would not tip it off as to my intentions. The tiles felt cold beneath my bare feet. Notwithstanding that the floor was dirty, I would eat the damned grape without washing it. Call it retribution.

I turned the light on, eradicating the womblike darkness, and searched on my hands and knees. But the grape was nowhere to be found. I suspected that it somehow must have sensed that it was best to make itself scarce. I had never been one to give credence to such metaphysical leanings, giving will and determination to inanimate objects, to food, but of late things hadn't been going so well in my life and it caused me to wonder; maybe Gaia, the Earth, was in fact a breathing sentient being. Maybe flowers or even the very food we ate had feelings. Who knew? I was looking for possibilities to get out from under the dark cloud that seemed to hover above me.

I peered under the fridge, the last place it could be, but couldn't spot it. I concluded, however, that it could only be under there, hiding at the far reaches.

I sat on a low stool and breathed deeply. The apartment was inordinately quiet, the silence only broken by the occasional humming of the fridge. As if ... as if ... the appliance and the grape were conspiring to drive me mad! And there I was, small, alone, very alone, slowly going off my rocker in the dead of night.

Suddenly I was filled with an intense emptiness. It didn't help that my wife had left me a few months earlier, having run off with a colleague she worked with. Surrounded as I was with darkness, with a sense of dread, all I wanted was to bury myself deep within the twisted blankets and sheets of my bed, close my eyes, and wait for the light of day. But now I had no choice, I had a problem and couldn't sleep until it was resolved. I would show my ex, I wasn't as pathetic as she no doubt thought. So I stood up, cursing all the while, and jerked mightily at the fridge. My back seized up.

"You've twisted your lower back," the doctor said the next day, palpating my lower back. "Technically, it's a lumbar strain. Stay off work for a week and relax. Eat well. I can write you a note if you need it." *Relax?* But I couldn't relax ... I could barely sleep as it was, and couldn't relax under any circumstance since the split. I was so uncomfortable, so distraught. I certainly couldn't eat. The thought of the grape lounging under the fridge dominated my every minute.

I paid the doctor $25 for his note and gingerly made it home, where I lay down onto the carpeted living room floor. Perspiration trickled down my hairline. There I stayed for what seemed like days, not washing, not eating not moving. Even breathing was a labour.

I made myself get up to make a sign. It was a sign on a piece of cardboard and it said: PLEASE HELP. It was too painful to write anything else—the pain seared like a long knife-blade twisting in my back—but I knew I could verbally explain to anyone who stopped that all I wanted was assistance moving the fridge.

I ambled to a street corner. "Excuse me," I said to passers-by, "I need your help." A few people gave me money but I couldn't engage anyone in conversation ... they just smiled or ignored me completely, and walked on by. Was it my unwashed hair? My rumpled clothes? The fact that I was in so much pain that my voice came out like a whisper?

Lost in thought and thoroughly upset, I stumbled to the next street, which happened to be under an overpass. Hunched over, I wanted to hand the money—$11.75—to a vagrant who was lying under his mattress, covered in blankets. I knew him, everyone in the neighbourhood did ... he was called *The Doctor* because for a small fee, he would dispense advice to anyone who wanted it ... and to some people who didn't. You always risked getting advice from The Doctor even if you walked right by him and didn't stop; he would simply shout out at you. "Be happy!" or "Take it easy!" or, perhaps the greatest bit of philosophical advice ever given—"Life is worth living!" … dime-store slogans to be certain.

Once he told someone to walk into traffic with his eyes closed but warned the gentleman, a very old man who I came to hear was on his last legs, wheezing and coughing, that he wouldn't be held liable if anything bad happened. So the guy did it, and nearly got killed. Sometimes the advice wasn't the best.

I heard all the stories about The Doctor from neighbours and shopkeepers. How exactly he got his moniker was something I didn't know, although I did hear one rumour that he had actually been a true-to-life doctor who had fallen on hard times. That seemed hard to believe. But it was true that he gave out advice. He had set up housekeeping under the overpass, complete with a mattress, pillows, blankets, a radio, candles, incense, a shopping cart filled with his clothes, piles of books in milk crates which he lent out to anyone who wanted, and a couple of lawn chairs. Sometimes when I'd walk by, I would see him sitting in one of the chairs, taking notes. Opposite would be *his patient*, I guess, someone who was looking for bad advice.

So I pushed on the pile of blankets and woke him. "Hey, get up," I said. "I need some advice."

"It'll cost you more because I'm sleeping."

Sleeping? How could he possibly sleep with the noise of passing cars? Not to mention all the grime and gunk.

"Not any more you're not," I said. "Besides, this is more important. *I* can't sleep." I emphasized the word 'I' to let him know he wasn't dealing with just anyone. "And my back is killing me, I can hardly stand, let along walk."

"You can't sleep? I've got something for you." The Doctor reached into a gym bag and pulled out a small bottle of gin. It was half empty. "Here," he said, thrusting it at me. "Two long slurps before bed. Now that'll be $2."

"$2? Your sign over there says: 'Free Advice. The Doctor is in. $1.'"

I had just now noticed the sign. Free advice and yet he was charging $1? And now he was charging me $2? That didn't make sense. But there it was, the clear contradiction in black marker on a piece of cardboard. It was obvious that he thought it was cute, having ripped it off from the Lucy character in the Charlie Brown comic strip.

"Like I said, I was sleeping when you called. You didn't even have an appointment. $2 please."

I handed over $2 from the $11.75.

"Giving me a half bottle of gin is bad advice," I said. "It won't solve my problems."

"I didn't say I give the best advice," he said. "Only that I give advice."

"Fair enough."

"You give up too easy. That might be your problem. Maybe why people don't like you. People don't like quitters, you know."

Sheesh. Did I really need this from this lunatic? I had passed the guy many times before and always suspected he was half-mad. And he certainly looked the part—his white hair was long and stringy, there was food stuck in his scraggly beard, his sweater was full of holes, and the smell that came off him ... oh my, like the sewer itself. No wonder he needed the incense, which he proceeded to light in my presence. But he was a fixture under the overpass, what with his crude cardboard sign that spoke of how hungry he was and how he had lost everything. In fact, I always dubbed him 'The Man Who Has Nothing.' Sometimes even 'The Man Who Lost It All.' I don't even know why I spoke to him now — it was apparent that life was no deeper for him than the bottom of the coffee cup where he collected change for his *services*.

"Maybe you have arachnophobia," he said, taking the gin from me and pulling up a lawn chair. "That's the fear of spiders. Many people are afraid of them."

"I know what it is and no, I don't have it."

The Doctor rose from his bed and sat in one of the lawn chairs, motioning for me to sit in the other.

"Maybe you might have a more serious problem," he said, writing something down in a notebook. "Maybe what you have is anthropophobia."

"What's that?"

"That's the fear of all people in all situations."

Hadn't I heard all this phobia stuff before? Like on a Charlie Brown TV show? I was sure of it, so I said so.

"Nope," The Doctor said. "It's all my own theories."

To save time, I explained my situation with the grape. The vagrant searched me with his grey eyes.

"What are you worried about?" he said at last, something slimy and awful slinking out his nose. He sputtered as he spoke, lifting his dirty forefinger up for emphasis. "All you have to do is wait for the aliens to show up. They'll help you, those little green guys. They can unlock the secrets to the universe. You know, sometimes you have to leave the complicated things to others."

Of course. Of course. What else could I expect! I looked at the man silently, seething, and thought I was an absolute dunce for soliciting advice from him, this man who had absolutely nothing. Truly, there was nothing there, not a single coherent thought in his warped brain.

But then he continued on: "Of course, you can always just leave the grape where it is. In time it will rot and disappear. Like everything."

"Interesting," I said.

"Or maybe a mouse will nibble away at it. Get the job done sooner. No matter, it will *vanish*." The Man Who Had Nothing placed great emphasis on the word 'vanish,' waving his hand in front of his face time and again like some crazed magician.

I gazed at the man with something now approaching respect. A little anyway.

"You make some sense," I said. "I hadn't thought about the rotting and disappearing, that time will take care of my problem. Or maybe a mouse will. But it's true. Aliens though, pah!" Of course, the rotting advice was something I could have figured out for myself … if only I hadn't been a complete wreck, sleepless and in agony.

"But tell me something," The Man Who Lost It All said. A Mack Truck rumbled by and he waited until it passed before continuing. "Anyway, why are you so concerned about a grape? It's hard to believe that anyone would lose sleep over that."

"No, you see, I was hardly sleeping even before the grape episode. My wife left me a while ago. And I seemed to be getting worse and worse every day. Then, when the grape decided to hide under the fridge, it just made my insomnia as bad as it could get. No sleep at all. Now my back hurts and that has been the final straw, not getting any shut-eye."

"Have you been to a doctor to see about your back?"

"Yes, he even gave me a note saying I should stay off work for a week. I paid him $25 for the note. God, everyone wants to make a buck off you."

"And so why can't you sleep? Is it all about your wife?"

I sighed deeply. I wasn't sure I could trust the man. Sure he now offered up some words of wisdom but certain secrets had pervaded my very essence, and I knew they might be disturbing to some. So I hesitated.

The Doctor continued on. "Well, let me ask you this. Why did your wife leave?"

"She ran off with someone she worked with."

"You sure about that?"

"What do you mean? What else?"

"Maybe there was no one else. Maybe she left because she didn't like what you had become."

"Well, look," I finally said, ready for the big reveal. "I'm an astronaut, you see, but I haven't been up into space in quite some time. And that depresses me. I love it in space. Anyway, the last time I was there, I saw a big blue UFO and reported it to NASA. It was kind of cigar-shaped and I could see two rows of windows. But they told me I was seeing Jupiter. Jupiter! Imagine that! It's not even blue!"

"I see," The Doctor said, closing his eyes in contemplation."

"Anyway, NASA told me to keep my mouth shut."

The Doctor started coughing, hacking like crazy, his

emaciated fake doctor's body shaking all over. He sputtered for a bit longer, saliva slipping out his mouth. It was disgusting. Finally his system calmed down and he began talking again, his voice barely above a whisper. "So you're not working now?"

"No."

"Why did you need a note from the doctor then?"

I hadn't thought about that. "You're trying to trip me up."

"No, I'm not. I'm trying to be logical. And help you."

"I'm not sure."

"Well, look, it appears you believe in aliens after all."

"Well, I guess I do."

The Man Who Lost It All looked me over, as if he were the teacher and I, a grade-school student in his class. Assessing. Maybe pondering if I were sane or not. I could see him watching my swinging leg. His head moved back and forth like a pendulum, back and forth in time to my leg. I didn't like it.

"Maybe you were never married in the first place," he said, looking directly at me. "Maybe you just made all that up. No wife. No. Maybe you can fool yourself but no one else, you know."

"I think I should go," I said, standing up. *What a snake.*

"Your time is just about up anyway. But come back any time." The Man Who Had Nothing walked over to a sewer grate where clouds of hot steam bubbled out. He lay down on top.

I started walking away.

"Think about the green aliens," he called out after me.

"You're an astronaut and you saw a spaceship so that means you're a believer, there's no doubt. There's life in everything. Everything beats with a heart."

Dead tired, I returned to my apartment, the very one that now felt warm and inviting. It was very strange. I prepared a hot meal of wieners and baked beans and ate voraciously. Then I closed the lights, curled up in bed beneath a mountain of soft blankets, and for the very first time in a long time, vanished deep into the abyss.

My insomnia seemed to get better from that day on, as did my back. I realized I owed my improved health to The Man Who Lost It All. The Man Who Had Nothing. So I thought I should go back and tell him how grateful I was for the advice. I even took out a bottle of vodka from the kitchen cupboard to give him as a gift. I knew he would like it, even if it was half-empty. But when I went to his subterranean office, he wasn't there. I returned a few more times but still he never showed. I finally asked one of my neighbours, someone cutting the front lawn.

"Get away from me," I was rudely told.

"You're not very nice," I said.

I tried asking a few other neighbours but everyone gave me a wide berth, ignoring me completely, like I had a terrible disease. Like the plague. People were so rude. Was it my unwashed hair? The fact that I hadn't changed my clothes? I didn't really feel like cleaning much, so maybe it was that? *The smell?* So I had no choice but to finally ask a vagrant in the neighbourhood.

"Oh, The Doctor," he said. "The guy who lived under the overpass. Well, he died a few weeks ago. I think he had emphysema."

The guy gazed at my bottle of vodka.

"You want this?" I said.

"Yes."

"Let me take a swig first. You can have the rest." The news of the death of The Man Who Had Nothing hit me hard.

I ventured down to the where the man had lived. All his things were still there. It seemed such a shame that everything would soon go to waste. All the doctor's working utensils. Unless ...

I took a black marker that I often kept in my back pocket and used it to change the sign that told of the services available. It now read: ice. *Free advice. The doctor is in. $2.00.*

Therapy wasn't cheap these days and besides, I could use the extra cash. Then I lit a stick of incense, lay down on the mattress, covered myself with blankets, and waited for my first patient.

It was a good plan to be out, on the periphery of all the revelry. Not exactly in the middle—there was an open-air party downtown but Lester knew that partying with strangers would have made him feel lonelier—but just on the cusp. A few doors down from where he would watch his laundry spin was a nightclub. Surely it would be rocking. Lester could absorb some of that ... sort of osmotically.

Nonetheless, for a forty-two-year-old man, it was all pretty grim. He was alone, so very alone on this most joyous night of the year. Lester, though, was determined to make an evening of it. He put on his best tweed jacket and straightened the knot on his tie. Dabbed a spot of cologne under each ear and tilted the wool cap on his head to a jaunty angle. On top of the laundry pile he placed a book, a bottle of sparkling water, and a large dark chocolate bar.

The night was glittering with frost as Lester headed up the street, carefully balancing the gift box in his arms. It was heavy, laden down with several weeks' worth of laundry. Ice crystals clung to his eyelashes and snow crunched under his boots. Up ahead he could make out the main street, a horizon of cafés and restaurants. Such a strange torment, a whole luminous world, no doubt buzzing with activity, but he, Lester Levine, barred from entry.

His destination was a subway ride away. There was a closer laundromat just up the road but that was a bit too near—any of his neighbours could walk by and see him. Lester lowered his face into the wind and his nostrils flared against the bitter cold. It would have been so much easier to stay at home, he realized. Easier but not better. Not that spending New Year's doing his laundry was great; far from it. But staying home alone was so much worse. Besides, he looked upon the excursion as an adventure—toying with the element of chance. An evening out without being spotted, a clandestine outing with an imaginary lover. Ah, it was all in good fun ... that was the best way to look at it.

The bluish glow of the streetlights illuminated the festive Christmas decorations on houses; it wasn't *his* holiday, he knew, but all the decorations and lights made Lester feel enervated nonetheless, glad to be alive, and he walked through the snow with renewed vigour.

On the crowded subway, Lester stood next to a young couple. Drunkenness had already overtaken them at this early hour of 8:30 pm and Lester could smell the liquor. They slurred their words and made funny faces at each other and Lester tried not to meet their eyes, focusing on an overhead ad for panty hose.

The Wash & Fold Laundromat was empty, a silent expanse of washing machines and dryers pitted against the joyous outside world by its starkness. Lester removed his coat and unwrapped the gift box. He placed the book along with the water and chocolate on top of a front-loading washing machine and began putting his clothes in. Sprinkled a cupful of detergent throughout and closed the door. Then he moved to the next machine and did the same. He searched a small leather coin purse he had brought for the exact change, sat back into a chair with his hands folded behind his head, and watched as the two machines throbbed to life.

Rotating clothes hypnotized him into a nostalgic reverie of holiday time. Family memories of Chanukah, menorahs, dreidels and latkes. Wife and daughter. A year and a half had now passed since his daughter died. An insidious fever of unknown origin. Four years old and life was over. The death had caused a rift between Lester and his wife, who blamed him. He understood she didn't need a reason, only that she needed someone to accuse. Despite that realization, Lester said nothing; he loved his wife and hoped she would come around on her own. But in the time since, he heard little from her and now divorce papers seemed inevitable. All the while, he grieved in silent resignation, his life shattered.

He stood up and ambled about the room, dabbing at his misty eyes. Someone had posted a sign for a musical group called 'Surrender Swine.' Heavy metal bangers. On a cork bulletin board, Lester read ads for reflexology, piano lessons, yoga classes, Sanskrit chanting and psychotherapy services.

He peered out through a clear patch in the frosted window and put his hand on the icy-cold pane. He could hear the music from the nightclub and started drumming in time on top of a dryer. "*Boom cha ka la ka boom boom boom* ..." He moved quickly from one machine to the next, rapping away and adding a few kicks for good measure. Suddenly he halted. The front door was being pushed open. A bundled-up figure wearing a toque with a scarf wrapped around the face and looking very much like an astronaut stepping onto Lester's small planet, trudged snow into the laundromat.

"Nasty out there. Cold."

Lester smiled but did not respond. He thought he should be cautious about engaging in conversation. *What sort of person did their laundry New Year's Eve?* Besides, he enjoyed having the place all to himself.

Hearing nothing in return, the woman looked up briefly and then quickly lowered her eyes. She opened the gym bag she had been carrying and began emptying the contents into a washing machine.

Lester sat back down and picked up his book. He would have liked to have eaten his chocolate bar. Now he couldn't—his evening was all ruined. He clenched his jaws tighter and tried to read but couldn't.

Lester snuck a peak at the woman. Then a second glance. Casual in sweats. Dark hair. Very pretty. Slowly and inexorably, a thought seeped into his mind and it caused Lester to reconsider matters. He realized that the woman's presence conferred a certain pleasantness onto this otherwise desolate laundromat. If initially he thought otherwise, it was only because the last year and a half of isolation had seeped into his very essence and made him wary of everyone. Like he was being fed arsenic by them.

His voice resounded with clarity in the silence that encapsulated the two: "Sorry to bother you," he said shyly, "but I was wondering if you might have a couple of quarters for this loonie. I usually do my laundry at home."

The woman, whose facial expression had been one of blank determination as she went about her business, smiled softly. "Sorry, I don't. Just brought enough to do my own laundry."

Lester shrugged. "I'll know better next time," he said. "If there is a next time. My machine at home is broken."

Lester didn't like the idea of lying but telling the truth was too complicated.

"Do you always do your laundry on New Year's Eve?" the woman asked playfully as she sorted her laundry. "All dressed up?"

"Well …" Lester stroked his chin and fell silent. He felt somewhat ashamed; despite his bravado that all was fine this special night, the question, no matter that it was asked in good humour, made him acutely aware of the gloomy situation he found himself in.

"Ah well, don't answer," the woman said, breaking the silence. "We end up doing laundry on New Year's for all sorts of reasons. Here I am as well."

The pronouncement took Lester by surprise and he broke into a smile. In short order both he and the woman were laughing.

"Diane Stollman." She extended a hand.

"Lester Levine. Would you like some dark chocolate?"

"Love some."

The two exchanged pleasant banter as a steady stream of people strode past the laundromat into the nightclub. Music and merriment … it was all beyond Lester's reach, separated not only by a frosty pane of glass but also by attitude and circumstance. But with each passing moment, it seemed to matter less and less. He was just as happy to be inside this lint-infested place, having made the acquaintance of a new, interesting woman. And, with a name like 'Stollman,' he suspected she was Jewish … an added bonus.

"Is that your gift box? Something left over from Christmas?"

"No, I actually brought my laundry in it," Lester said sheepishly. "Kind of a long story."

"I have nowhere to go."

So Lester revealed his hangup about being seen carrying a laundry basket New Year's Eve.

"I understand completely," Diane said. "We all have our issues."

Issues. Lester had his and felt the need to unburden himself. "How is it that an intense love can unravel completely and turn to dust?" he said suddenly.

"Whoa, that's a big one. Sure you want to go there?"

"You're right. Why don't we shift gears. Tell me—why is a nice lady like you doing laundry tonight?"

"Well, I had a couple of parties to go to but decided tonight would be good downtime. I suffer from adrenal fatigue, which means I get tired easily and have to pace myself."

"Adrenal fatigue?"

"It's one of those things that comes about because of a lot of stress,. Unremitting stress. Eventually your body puts the brakes on your 'always-on-the-go' lifestyle."

Diane took a bite of chocolate. "I shouldn't have this. Sweets aren't good for those with adrenal problems. But what the heck—I'm celebrating New Year's ... here in the laundromat."

"With a stranger."

"Not any more."

For the next hour, Lester and Diane talked and time slipped away. They shared an interest in foreign film and literature and Lester's book caught her interest: *The Curious Incident of the Dog in the Night-Time*. "What a strange title!"

"It is but the story itself is quite unique, about a very odd boy who takes it upon himself to investigate the death of a neighbourhood dog."

For the first time in years, Lester found himself with a person who took him away from his problems, out of his habit of rehashing his internal dissonances. He felt so comfortable in fact, that he even admitted that he had lied about the quarters.

"Full of quarters," he said, opening the change purse and jingling the coins about.

As the magic hour loomed, Lester wondered how to extend the evening. The clothes were tumbling softly in the dryers and would be ready shortly. It then came to him, an inspired idea that caused him to suddenly blurt out: "Diane, you've got this interest in literature and well, I have a published piece. A short story that appeared in a magazine called 'Drash.'"

"If you don't mind me saying, that's a strange name for a magazine."

"It's a west coast magazine from Seattle. The name comes from a Jewish word meaning 'to tell'."

"That makes sense then. What's the story about?"

"Really?"

"Sure."

"Ok, well, it's the story of a man whose fiancée dies. He's so distraught that he can barely function, life now seems meaningless. So he goes to a rabbi schooled in Kaballah, the mystical aspect of Judaism, and basically pleads with him—he literally gets on his hands and knees—to help him erect a golem in the image of his fiancée. He just wants to see her once again. To tell her he loves her."

"What a great premise."

"I'd like to share it with you. I mean, let you read it."

"Of course. That'd be great."

"Then I'll be back in twenty-five, maybe thirty minutes," said Lester, throwing on his coat.

"You mean you're going home to get it *now*?!"

"No time like the present," Lester said. "Why don't you read the Dog book and enjoy the chocolate. Stay right there."

Outside, Lester tried hailing a cab to no avail and then decided to run, all eighteen blocks. He could have taken the subway but running was faster, even in the blustery weather.

The air was cold and his boots big and clumpy but it didn't matter in the least to Lester. He darted around people and picked up the pace with each passing block, careful to avoid patches of ice. By the time he reached home, his ears were red and his lips numb. He collapsed onto the couch, his chest heaving.

Diane had just finished folding her clothes when she saw a terrible face pressed up against the window. Then a second. And a third.

The men stomped inside, drunk and loud. "Hey little lady," one said. "What're you doin' with yourself here? In this here dump all by your lonesome."

"Leave me alone. You're drunk."

"Oh, ho! A live one."

One of the men grabbed Diane. "Dance with me, beautiful," he commanded. "Let's celebrate. It's New Years!" She broke free and tried to throw on her coat but was re-strained.

"Let's see what the lady's reading." The tallest of the three men, with icicles in his long unkempt beard, picked up the book and leafed through the pages. "Listen to this boys: *'A lie is when you say something happened which didn't happen.'* No shit! This is for morons. Grade 5 stuff."

He waved the book in front of Diane's face. "You finish grade 5 little lady?"

"I'm sure you haven't," she responded bravely.

The man grasped Diane's arm with his great yellowed hands and squeezed.

"You're hurting. Let go."

"Ah, let her go," one of the man's companions said.

"Can I have my book back," Diane said tersely.

The man with the beard strode up to her so that they were face-to-face. "You're testing my patience, little lady. Here. You want da book?" He held it in front of her belea-guered eyes. "Go get it then."

The man then deliberately ripped the book and threw it in the wastebasket.

He removed a small bottle of gin from inside his coat, took a long swig and passed it to his friends.

"Lucky woman," he murmured.

Tears welling in her eyes, Diane hurriedly put on her coat, grabbed her gym bag full of clothes and left the laun-dromat, followed shortly thereafter by the men.

☙

Lester departed his house, a copy of the magazine he had come for rolled up in his coat pocket. His legs felt heavy but the compelling thought that he would meet up with Diane again spurred him to march briskly back to the laundromat. Every now and then the wind picked up, lacing his face with snow, and causing him to slow.

When at last he entered into the Wash & Fold Laundromat, he found it as empty as an interstellar black hole. He saw the torn up book in the trash and realized that he had deluded himself. There was no doubt. How pathetic it seemed now — how utterly stupid — to have run home in the cold to fetch a magazine for some stranger. He really was a loser.

He languidly removed his clothes from the dryers. The chocolate was still there and for a moment, he considered putting it back into his gift box; instead he flung it into the garbage. He looked at his watch and took a deep breath. If he could find a cab, he would take it. He knew that if he hurried, he could make it home just in time to bring in the New Year with *Dick Clark's New Year's Rockin' Eve*.

THE UNDERGROUND CIRCUS

THE CIRCUS CAME to town. It came in the middle of the night, with only the town drunks to greet the caravan. It came in buses and trucks and cars and vans. Why, even two rickety wagons arrived, pulled by majestic white horses. Of course, because it arrived when most everyone was fast asleep, no one could do anything about it. The ensemble just drove into town with their animals and assorted acts and declared that they were there to stay for an indefinite period of time. Not even the mayor had any say over the matter. It seemed that the circus reigned supreme.

Of course, it was the people themselves who really wanted it, from town to town, city to city, patrons who were willing to pay big bucks. That wasn't too surprising. When the main act is a young boy who refuses to come down from the high wire, well, it goes without saying that a lot of people would be interested.

And so the impresario of the World's Biggest Circus, one Fergus McDuff, a short, rotund man with red veins running like bloody tributaries across his bulbous nose, emerged early one evening from the flap of the canvas tent with a sweep of his arm.

"Never again will you folks be witness to such a spectacle!" he bellowed into his megaphone. "Never! So come one and come all and see this incredible event! Right this way, ladies and gentlemen, right this way!"

The large crowd, which had been gathering for hours under a scorching sun, now pushed forward.

"All proceeds to charity," a smiling McDuff said, and he held out a wooden bucket into which willing patrons plunked their money.

One by one the seats filled up. The audience laughed when the clowns came on and gasped when an overexcited lion took a real swipe at his handler, slicing his shoulder. Generally though, the crowd was impatient. This was not what they had come to see.

So they scornfully hooted and hollered at the performer who was able to keep six plates spinning on six different poles and threw peanuts at the sword swallower, aiming for his open mouth.

It hadn't always been this way. At one time, the circus had very much belonged to all of its various performers. The strong man who could pull a two-ton bus was a major attraction. So too was the wolf lady whose entire forehead was covered with hair. The two-headed man, Jack and Ivan, whose heads hated each other and who would conduct public shouting matches, was a popular figure. The lion tamers, trampoline artists, clowns, jugglers, tumblers, fire-eater, skeleton woman, fat boy, and the rest ... they had all attracted their fair share of attention. But no longer. Now they were mere annoyances to the throngs who came out to see a much more important act.

And so, through sheer strength of will, these artists continued with their routines, routines which should have been easy for them but were not. The strong man had great difficulty pulling the bus each time out—in fact, the seats inside had to be removed so as to lighten his load. One of the trampoline artists injured his neck in a fall, having completed only 2½ of his 3 mid-air backward somersaults. The sword swallower had to be hospitalized for perforating his oesophagus. And so it went.

Perhaps to deny their own feelings would have served them best, yet for most of the performers, it was impossible to do so. For far too long had they been deities in the eyes of the circus audiences—it was only natural that they would feel resentful and bitter. McDuff had his hands full keeping his troops at bay. At one point or another, each and every performer, save one, threatened to pack it in. Although if truth be known, these were simply idle threats designed to attract attention to their plight. Where else, for instance, could the strong man have worked if not in a circus ring? It is true that on one occasion he did venture into the centre of one city where he managed to hitch his harness to a bus, thereby attracting a sizable crowd. And while it is also true that he pulled that bus for nearly a kilometre through the city streets with great ease—much to the amazement of passers-by—it is significant to note that he was not paid a penny for his troubles and in fact slapped with a seventy-five dollar fine by the local courts for obstructing traffic, who thought his act not amusing in the least.

A stray glance here and there from the public was not enough. Yet it was all the artists could realistically hope for. They were competing against someone who was bigger than them, someone seemingly bigger than the circus itself.

The *insane man*, as McDuff liked to refer to him, packed them in. And it was because of him that the tight-fisted impresario could offer his disgruntled cast a few more dollars as compensation for their misery. But he didn't. He did just the opposite. He made them take pay cuts.

"You can leave," he told each and every one of them. "Try to catch on with another circus." He had them and knew it. For various reasons, the interest in traditional circuses had diminished over the years and jobs were hard to come by. Now it was all about circuses that blended choreography and art and rock shows—spectacles like Cirque du Soleil.

So when the lights dimmed and the spotlights shone upwards to the high wire, the entire cast of circus performers listened sadly to the wild applause that had once rightly belonged to them. Now they could only retire quietly to the anonymity of their dressing rooms, where they would recall past glories with the aid of yellowed newspaper clippings.

It was this very high wire performer that everyone had now come to see. A tall, willowy man with sunken cheeks, wisps of fine red hair, and a straggly red beard that resembled a robin's nest, he was their idol. To say that Belon's act—or lack of one, to be more precise—was unusual, would certainly understate the case. For it wasn't so much an act as an opportunity for patrons to be a part of something grandiose and certainly unique.

As for the wire, it hovered one-hundred-and-twenty-seven feet above the ground and that in itself was not so unusual; indeed, it was only slightly higher than high wires at other circuses. Nor was it Belon's balanced walk from one perch to the other along that same fine wire that lured the crowds—there was nothing extraordinary about it. In fact, Belon had performed this very walk hundreds of times.

No, it was more than that—a glimpse into the internal machinations of some strange genius perhaps. And to that end, it was only when the walk ended that the audience would begin its rhythmic clapping. This was obviously the beginning of what all had come to see.

"Wash them! Go ahead and wash them!" was the cry that reverberated throughout the circus tent. And it was usually not long after the spectators' chant climbed upward to his illustrious perch that Belon would begin his ritual.

First, he would sit down and remove his well-worn slippers. Then he would reach for a wooden pail that was strategically situated on an abutment above the wooden perch he sat on. Inside the pail was water, a bar of soap and a washcloth, items he needed to wash his feet.

As Belon washed, droplets of soapy water would rain down to the circus floor where feverish patrons stood waiting with bowls or cups or pots ... any device, in fact, in which to catch a few drops of what had become known as Belon's Holy Water.

The water was said to have miraculous medicinal

qualities—everything from warts to blindness to paralysis was thought to have been cured with it. As testimony to its veracity, McDuff erected a makeshift shed within the circus tent that housed the discarded crutches, canes, and other such aids which true believers left behind.

After he had washed, Belon would begin his sermon. With microphone in hand, he would talk about things like unconditional love, good and evil, forgiveness, and about having ultimate faith in God. The talks would usually last ten minutes, no longer, and during those moments all the lighting in the tent was turned off, with the exception of a solitary candle which Belon himself would light. Viewed from down below, it gave him the appearance of something other-worldly; the unusual luminosity made him look transparent, ethereal.

"We're all God's children," he would begin in a voice that was full of passion. "He loves all of us the same. A beggar on the street, the head of a corporation. It doesn't matter."

At this point, he would usually put his slippers back on and take a short walk along the wire, holding the candle in front to light the way. The effect was dramatic—with Belon swathed in darkness, it looked as if the candle was moving of its own accord. Back on his perch, his head bowed, he would go into a trance-like state and his voice would change, becoming more melodic, calmer. There was a ring of wisdom and understanding to it, a sacrosanct voice, of a higher being addressing his flock.

"Many of you think that you will be met by a tribunal upon your death. A group of wise men will sit in judgment of you, of all the things you have done in this lifetime. Let me assure you know that there is no such tribunal. The truth is that you will be bathed in an awesome light when you pass and you will come to know that you are one with the Lord. You will know love as you have never known it before. You will shed all illusion, and you will know that you are Home ..."

He would always end the same way: "While I cannot come down to be with you at this time, you are all free to join me up here."

Two strong men hired by McDuff would then take their places at the foot of the rope ladder leading up to the high wire, where they would ward off screaming and frenzied patrons wanting to climb up to Belon's exalted perch.

After his oration, Belon would blow out the candle and bed down for the evening on his perch. He was quite tall, about six feet two inches, and since the platform was only five feet square, sleeping was a problem for him. For the most part, to ensure his safety, he slept curled up and attached a harness around his waist; the other end he attached to the pole.

As for his other needs, an engineer was brought in to devise a pulley system, so that both his food and wastes moved up and down with ease.

Belon was born Belon Munchhauser to parents he never knew. His father was a lifetime thief, specializing in stealing high-end cars like Mercedes and Volvos that were shipped overseas. Belon was three when the old man was stabbed to death in prison. Belon's mother was a stripper, or a 'dancer' as she liked to call herself. After her husband's death, she ran off with a client, leaving the child in the care of her mother's sister, Aunt Emm.

Emm had her own problems. She was diagnosed as an obsessive-compulsive who had a morbid fear of germs. She made Belon a pair of plastic wraps out of Saran Wrap for his feet and made him wash his hands exactly twelve times before a meal. Her own hands she washed fifteen times. By the time he was seven, Belon's hands were raw and bloody and he had difficulty holding a pencil. That would have been a problem had the child gone to school, but Belon never did. Emm didn't believe in schools.

When he was nine, Belon escaped from Emm's asylum in upstate N.Y. He was offered a ride by a trucker who was transporting a load of sheep. It was the first time Belon had ever touched an animal and he was so enamoured with the softness of their wool, that he slept in the back with them, snuggled amidst the fleece.

"I can take you to Chicago. That's where I'm goin'. I've got a buddy there who's goin' to St. Louis. Got some of them free range chickens to deliver. If ya wanna go with him, you can go with him. He's goin' to St. Louis, like I said."

The ride with the chickens was not as pleasant. They roamed freely in the back of the truck. "Not allowed to keep 'em in cages. That's why theys called *'free range'*." There was no room for Belon in the front since the trucker used the remaining seat for his Bull Mastiff dog. "Travels with me everywhere. Good company."

The chickens squawked constantly, bitter old hags. They defecated on the boy and pecked at his raw hands until they started oozing blood. Their feathers flew into Belon's mouth and ears.

He was let off in St. Louis and wandered the streets, foraging for food in back alleys.

Street urchin, uneducated dirty boy ... bound to live in abject poverty, bound to taste life's bitter handouts: begging, cold, booze, gangs, unemployment, no love. Another victim. End of story.

But wait, a saviour arrives for the boy. Someone promising to take care of him. Food. A home. Chance for a better life.

"You've got good tone," McDuff said, rubbing his palms. "A bit skinny, but a fine specimen."

"Don't you touch me, mister." That free-range chicken-traveling boy of nine has turned into a steely street youth of eleven. He carries a switchblade in his back pocket. His red hair is shaven in a buzz cut. He wears Doc Martens. He has a tattoo of a Swastika on his right shoulder blade.

"Have you ever heard of the World's Biggest?" McDuff said.

"Yah, and I'm lookin' at 'im now, Mister."

"McDuff's the name. My friends call me *Duffie*." He handed his card to the boy, who shoved it away.

"Piss on it. Can't read and write, Mister."

"I run the World's Biggest Circus. Always looking for young men to join. Are you scared of heights?"

Belon didn't answer. Instead he pulled out a flask of brandy from beneath his coat and took a swig. It made him grimace.

"Look, tell you what, m'boy. Tonight's our last night

in this here town. Then we move on to Orleans. We're havin' a big feast after the show ... starts around eleven. Come round back of the tent, ask for me. You can meet some of the circus acts. What's your favourite? You like clowns? Lions? Hey, I know, you go for them high-wire acts, I can tell."

McDuff stroked his chin in contemplation. "Tell you what. Maybe you'd like to see the show? Got a ticket right here. Third row. That's not bad." He carefully handed Belon the ticket. "You've still got them freckles, m'boy." He tweaked the boy's nose and started ambling away.

"I CAN STILL CUT YOU, MISTER!"

That was twenty years ago. Under the tutelage of *The Great Waldo* (everyone at the *World's Biggest Circus* went by the name of *The Great* or *The Amazing*), that street smart boy turned into a world class high-wire walker. He rode a bicycle across the wire, walked the length of it backwards, ate his lunch on it, crawled across it, ran across it, did two-handed handstands on it, did one-handed handstands on it, walked across it blindfolded, and generally, performed with the wire to such an extent and in such an intimate fashion that it became a part of his life, his very essence, and he was unable to imagine a life apart from the wire. He was *The Amazing Belon, High-Wire Walker*—that's precisely who he was.

Then, sometime after his thirtieth birthday, something changed in Belon. He grew restless, dissatisfied with his life. Perhaps it was the constant travelling, the low pay, the fact that he had no friends outside the circus. He couldn't quite put his finger on it. But this inner churning, this vague torment, rankled, and left him sleepless.

"What is it, m'boy? McDuff still called him *m'boy* after all these years. "You look like Bubba the Elephant, all puffy-like, bloated."

"Can't sleep."

"Is Fat Christine still after you? If she's a knockin' on your trailer late at night, disturbin' you, I'll let her have it … if you know what I mean."

"No, it ain't her."

McDuff puffed on a fat cigar, blowing cumulus clouds into the air.

Belon glanced at McDuff. He noticed that a vein had burst on his nose, a pinch of blood trickling out. He rarely ever looked at McDuff. Now he noticed how old he appeared. Still a trickster, still the *sham man* as he was known within the circus, but an aging one. He hardly resembled the man who had picked him up on those streets of St. Louis all those years ago. The longer he looked at him, and the more he thought about how he had spent his entire life within the small world of circus performers, amongst freaks, animals, and clowns, with no real family to call his own, the more that hazy torment crystallized for Belon. Although he couldn't put it into so many words and express those thoughts and feelings, he now understood why he was feeling the way he was.

I'm the Amazing Belon, but I could be that smoking man, he thought to himself.

It was arranged that Belon would see a social worker. Although McDuff didn't really care whether his employees were happy or not, he didn't want them quitting. He could always get out-of-work performers to replace them, but it was too much of a hassle breaking new people in. So he agreed to let Belon talk to someone, get his troubles out.

The circus had an indefinite stay in San Francisco anyway, probably months. Small crowds were expected but any stay longer than a week was surprising ... and most welcome. It was agreed then that Belon would see her once a week, on Monday mornings, when the circus wasn't performing.

Penny Singer, M.S.W., fifty-six, never married, had her shingle located on the top floor of a run-down Victorian house in an older part of the city. She occupied a small room next to an aesthetician salon, overlooking a vacant warehouse that was sometimes used by vagrants. She had once been a partner in *Singer, Spelling, and Thompson*, located in the heart of the downtown business core. She and her partners were renowned for getting burnt-out executives back to work and for giving seminars to corporations about improving employee moral.

A number of years ago, however, there had been a falling out with Spelling and Thompson because she insisted on seminars relating to spirituality in the workplace.

There were also allegations from a fifteen-year-old boy that Penny had touched him. It all became too much for Spelling and Thompson and they bought out Penny's interest in the partnership.

Attracted by the lyrical name *Penny Singer*, McDuff had found her in the Yellow pages. Besides, she worked for cheap. *Penny for pennies*, McDuff told Belon.

"When I was a little girl, I always thought of running away and joining the circus. But there was something about the circus that scared me."

"Nuthin' to be scared about."

"Oh, I know. But I think it was the clowns that scared me. You know, the make-up."

Penny lit a cigarette. "Mind if I smoke?"

Belon shook his head. He saw that the social worker's fingertips were yellow.

"What brings you here?"

"I came by bus."

Penny laughed. "No, I mean—why have you come to see me?"

Belon was entirely sober. "It's not so easy to ... ugh ... you know, say what's on my mind."

"Well, I had the chance to speak a bit about you with your boss, Mr. McDuff. He said you might be depressed. Are you depressed?"

"I dunno."

"I'll make something clear right away, Belon. You're

going to have to talk to me if we're going to get anywhere. You're going to have to trust me. Do you trust me?" She moved from behind the oak desk and pulled up a chair next to Belon. Then she held one of his large hands between hers. "You do trust me, don't you?"

Belon's back arched instinctively. He would have liked to back his own chair away, but his hand was stuck in hers. He felt nervous. He had never been this close to a regular woman before. The only woman who had ever touched him before was Sexy Sadie, the circus' tattooed lady. He felt his erection growing and tried to cover it with his free arm.

"Well, I'll try," he replied.

"Good, good, that's a start." She rose and sauntered to a small kitchen counter near the window. "Can I get you a coffee or tea?"

"Coffee."

With her back turned to him, Belon felt at liberty to watch Penny. He could see the outline of her bra beneath her white blouse. He looked at her legs, which were somewhat muscular, but quite well-defined. They reminded him of Shawna's, the woman who worked the trampoline and whom Belon had long had a crush on. He continued sizing her up, her waist with the love handles that he could see gently pushed out the sides of her blouse, her thick black hair with the speckles of grey in it that was tied tightly into a bun. She was only maybe five feet four inches, but for some reason she seemed to him much taller, like she was walking not on her real legs but rather on stilts.

Over the next few weeks, Belon gradually began to open up. He had never before had the chance to talk about his feelings and thoughts. He told Penny about how *Duffie* picked him up on the streets of St. Louis and introduced him to the circus, about how he was grateful to the impresario for having done so, but that he didn't want to end up like his boss. He wanted more from life, but didn't know exactly what that was. He did know that he wanted a better home than just a trailer, maybe a wife and kids, maybe a regular job. Although he could read (Child Welfare made sure that all children in circuses received private tutoring up to age sixteen), he couldn't write very well. "I'd like to learn better," he said.

Five weeks after they started their sessions, Penny told Belon that *she* felt misunderstood and often lonely. It was a remark out of the blue.

"I'm comfortable with you," she said, sighing. "It's been a long time since I've met a man I could say that about." She glanced at him with her head cocked sideways, a little unsure.

Belon smiled a somewhat toothless smile. He didn't like showing his teeth as he was missing two of them from rot.

"Do you like this?" She took his massive hand and put it on her breast.

"Oh," said Belon uncertainly. He tried to move his hand away but she held it there firmly.

"But Ms. Singer ..." he protested lamely.

She kissed him. It was a long, slow kiss, and her tongue parted his reluctant teeth and roamed wildly about his cavernous mouth. With that, he could resist no longer.

Every atom in his body succumbed to the sheer pleasure and he sprawled with Penny onto the floor, his mouth and hands groping for flesh. He sucked and stroked and gave as much as he received. All at once, he became a veteran in the arena of love, knowing exactly how to move, how to touch.

Breathless, she suddenly pushed his wild mouth off hers. "See how the furniture is arranged in this office," she said, laughing. "I arranged it myself. It's based on the ancient Chinese art of Feng Shui."

Belon wasn't listening. He was moving his lips down her luscious neck. He was gnawing at her clavicle when she pushed him up again.

"Energy has to be able to flow freely. You can't put any furniture in the way. It'll just block the flow. You have to arrange things to create the most positive flow of energy."

Belon kissed her mouth, hoping to keep her quiet.

"Enjoy," he muttered.

She pushed him up again, this time more forcefully.

"See that plant over there," she said. Belon turned on his elbows to look at the jade plant. "I used to have it near the door. Then I realized that it interfered with the movement of energy in the office. So I moved it next to the window. I felt better after that. More grounded."

Belon didn't comprehend. "I don't know what you're talking about," he said, as a long spittle of drool cascaded from his mouth.

"I'm nervous," she said. "It's been so long." She pushed his big lug of a body away.

"I think I understand," Belon said softly, and he put his arm around Penny's shoulder.

The next few weeks went well for Belon. He spent every Monday morning wrapped in Penny's arms and legs. Somehow though, the intimacy mitigated against him revealing his most intimate thoughts. He was Penny's lover now. He didn't want to be her patient. So after their lovemaking sessions were over, he would spend the remaining time listening to *her*. She had much to say and in between stealing kisses, he would listen with interest, not always understanding. Penny spoke about God and Lucifer, and generally about 'spiritual stuff' as Belon would say. He liked listening to her ramble on. He rarely spoke. The arrangement was just fine.

It so happened that on one occasion, the arrangement became … not so fine. Belon felt a need to talk and told Penny as much.

"Ok, what do you want to talk about?"

"It's kind of why I came here in the first place, sweetcakes. I ain't happy at work and no amount of lovin' is gonna change that."

Penny thought for a moment, her eyes twinkling.

"I've got it!'

"Got what?!"

"What to do about your job!" she said.

The plan that Penny hatched in her spiritually-bent brain was this: Belon would stay up on his high wire perch, live up there, and give sermons on all things spiritual. He would touch deep chords in people. She told him: "In these grossly materialistic times, people are dying for some spiritual guidance. They want to nourish their souls. There's a whole lost generation looking for itself."

He would become known as a prophet, a messiah. The word of God would speak through him. Amen. She would orchestrate the whole thing. She, of course, would be the only one allowed up to visit him. She would come in a cherry picker (she was too old to climb the rope ladder) and provide him with the daily sermons he would read. His reading was good enough for that. They would practice. No one would know. They would think that she was there to support him. She was a social worker, after all.

"But if you write like you, people will know I didn't write those sermons. I don't speak so good as you write."

"That's the whole point!" she exclaimed, smiling. "Everyone knows you speak badly. So how come you're able to talk so well when you give your orations? It's because God is speaking through you! You're just his instrument!" She pointed her finger at him. "You can pretend to go into a trance and voila — you're *Belon the Great Prophet!*"

Penny softly stroked Belon's cheek. "My beloved," she said.

The *World's Biggest Circus'* extended stay in San Francisco lasted exactly three months and twenty-two days, far exceeding any normal run. It ended rather abruptly when the mayor of the city advised McDuff that the town council had taken a vote—it was unanimously agreed that Belon was having a bad influence on San Francisco's children. Many such impressionable youngsters were following Belon's lead, remaining up in trees and on rooftops and any other high perch they decided upon, proclaiming that they would not come down under any circumstances ... well, at least not until their hero did. City counsellors were deluged with phone calls from frantic parents and the ghastly wail of the city's firetrucks could be heard throughout the days and nights.

The trouble was that Belon didn't want to come down. He was happy where he was. He liked the attention and Penny had negotiated for him a sparkling deal with McDuff, based upon a generous share of the circus' revenues. He didn't want for anything, Penny made sure of that. Even his bi-weekly trysts with her, concealed under the veil of late evening darkness and within the boom basket, were dandy. Granted, there wasn't a lot of room to manoeuvre. Standing up was the best method.

With Penny not around, McDuff sent one of the trampoline artists to go up and fetch the madman. But it didn't work. When he got quite close to the high wire, Belon began gently prodding him in the chest with his fibreglass pole, until the trampoline artist thought for sure that he would lose his grip on the rope ladder and tumble down. He quickly scurried down of his own accord. Then it was one of the strongmen who was sent up. And after that the sword swallower. Belon's dexterity with the pole continued to serve him well. McDuff himself was the last to try but he only got about halfway up before he froze with fear —he had never been that high before.

The impresario then thought the best way to combat his star attraction was to beat him at his own game, make other acts more attractive. The problem was that the acts he had were well-worn, and not that unusual. He needed something different, something no other circus had. So he decided on jousting. Not just a regular joust where no one got hurt. No, this was the real deal, where participants used swords, or other weapons, and where the blood was real. This was the Roman Coliseum all over again, with one main difference—the individuals jousting were children. That was the main catch, a bloody fight using street kids that had nothing to lose, whose demise no one cared about.

McDuff rubbed his hands with glee. *It'll go over like wildfire!* he thought. *And no one will think the more of stupid Belon. He'll come down himself and that'll be that.*

That was the plan, and it worked for a bit, once exactly. McDuff found two ruffians. One was rummaging for food in a dumpster, the other begging for change. One was fourteen, the other sixteen. Just as he had once done with Belon, he gave them tickets to the show, fed and housed them, introduced them all around. Then he showed them how to use a sword and a lance, a flail, and anything else he could uncover at army surplus stores, any place that sold medieval wares. He outfitted the combatants with slim body armour but the arms and legs were exposed. He promised them all manner of wealth and fame, if only they would fight. And fight they did. Before a packed house. It was violent and bloody and patrons were shocked, but they egged on the boys, although some people walked out in horror. Skin was ripped, screams rampant. Each time one of the boys fell, wriggling in pain, McDuff got a circus performer to prop him up. It lasted just long enough for the police to arrive, shut down the circus, take the combatants to the hospital, and arrest McDuff.

When he was let out on bail the next day, the impresario was surly. Now he faced possible jail time and a substantial fine, and in his mind, he attributed it all to Belon. He got his band of swashbuckling rogues together.

"Hi ho, hi ho, buckaroos!" he said. "I'm mad as hell. The blowhard's under my skin and I'm not gonna take it anymore!"

McDuff turned to Sylvie, the Lizard Woman. Owing to some congenital birth defect (it was rumoured that her father was a reptile), her entire body was covered with greenish scaly skin. "Well, darlin'. Do you know what we do when someone in the circus doesn't toe the line?"

Sylvie bit her lip. A crust of skin under her vermillion border flaked off onto the ground.

"We make them walk the plank, that's what!" McDuff screamed, now sounding like Captain Hook. "Give 'em the ride of their lives, maties!"

With the exception of Sexy Sadie, who held up a single finger, no one objected. They had grown tired of Belon, the show-stealer, the usurper of the limelight. And many felt that the fight was truly despicable, attributable solely to him ... McDuff could spin a good story that the bout had been Belon's idea. His alone.

McDuff got into Sadie's face. "Now I know you have a soft spot for him," he said, looking her straight in the eyes. "But you see this, Sexy Lady?" He pulled 10 one hundred dollar bills from his back pocket and dramatically spun around, holding the bills high in the air." This belongs to each and every one of you, if you keep your mouths shut!"

He turned again to the tattooed lady. "What do you say, honey-bun?"

Sadie nodded. "Okay, Duffie."

With those delicious words, the impresario stuffed the bills into Sexy Sadie's cleavage.

"It's this way ..." he whispered to his assembled band.

It was decided that Shawna would scale the rope ladder at the far end of the high wire, opposite Belon's perch. She would do this late at night, when Belon was fast asleep. She would then cut the wire slightly, but enough that a few more walks across it would unravel it completely.

There were advantages to using Shawna as the perpetrator. She, of course, was quite unafraid of heights, given that she worked the trampoline. There was also the possibility that Belon might awaken during the escapade. If that happened, she could use her feminine wiles to explain away the climb. "It's been so long since I saw you close-up," she would declare. "I miss you." Everyone was aware of Belon's infatuation for her.

Extraordinarily large crowds came out to see Belon over the next few days. Standing room only. People heard that the circus had been forced to leave and many devotees took the opportunity to view *the man* one last time. It was reasonable to assume that many intended to follow Belon to whatever city or town he moved to. Still, for many it would be the last time.

Three days after the most devious act (it had been done in the wee hours of the morning, on an evening when Belon and Penny had had a particularly rigorous love-making session, which left him dead-tired), and on his 6th walk along the wire, it snapped like a whip and Belon tumbled unmercifully to the hard ground below, some one hundred and twenty-seven feet.

There was a mad rush to attend to the fallen man, as shocked patrons cried for their hero. McDuff was ready, however. He had hired a dozen out-of-work strongmen to handle the crowds. "It's our affair," he yelled. Only Sexy Sadie attended the stricken man. She cradled his head and wiped the blood from his nose and eyes. He moaned a couple of times, smiled briefly at Sadie, and then was still.

When Penny found out, she wept inconsolably. It was a full three days before she was able to compose herself enough to venture down to the circus, where she saw it packing up to move on. She tried to wrangle some answers from the circus performers, only to find out that no one knew how the accident happened. They all said the same thing: Either the wire accidentally broke, sending Belon spiraling downward, or else Belon himself slipped off the wire and his fall caused it to snap on his way down. Penny asked to see the wire but McDuff said he had disposed of it in the trash. As for the body, it was sent to the funeral parlour.

When Penny arrived at *Johnson & Son's Funeral Parlour*, she got in line with Belon's followers. It took her close to two hours before she was able to view the body and when she finally did, she collapsed onto his chest and had to be physically removed from the corpse.

Outside, she was met by Sexy Sadie.

"I thought you might be here. I couldn't talk at the circus, you understand."

When Sadie was finished, Penny bit her knuckle and wept onto her knees.

That night, under the pretence of delivering a basket of chocolates and other munchies that some adoring fan had sent, Penny returned to the circus and found McDuff in his trailer. The impresario opened the door a crack and was greeted with a knife to the head. He collapsed backward against a dresser as blood splashed onto the floor from the open wound.

"We can talk about this!" he screamed, backing up as Penny burst through the door. He frantically sought his last refuge—his unmade bed.

"You're an asshole and now you're going to die!" She took a long vicious swipe but missed.

"Okay, kill me if you want. But first listen!"

Penny contemplated the impasse. McDuff was cowering at the far reaches of the bed and she was on the floor; in order to knife him she'd have to jump onto the bed. She reached over as far as she could and again took a mad swing—yes, he was definitely out of reach.

"Speak, asshole! But make it quick!"

"Heaven help Belon! He was a good man!'

"He was my man!"

"That he was ... that he was." He put his hand to the forehead—he couldn't see anymore. "My eyes, my eyes," he said, trying in vain to wipe away the flowing blood.

She was disarmed by his helplessness. She couldn't help it. She went for a rag at the sink and threw it at him.

"There's turpentine on this," he said, wincing.

She got another rag, a clean one, and wet it with water. Again she threw it. It smacked into his face with a *thwack*.

"Look, no one wanted to see Belon die," McDuff said. "We just wanted to scare him a little, that's all. I don't give one goddamn what anyone told you."

"How do you know what someone told me?!" she said.

"I don't, I don't."

"Look, see this knife here? In a minute, I'm going to throw it on the bed. I want you to pick it up and slit your own throat. And don't think about using it on me. I've got a pistol in my purse, asshole!"

Penny moved her right hand into her purse and kept it there.

The impresario cowered in the corner. He dare not pick up the knife.

"Please," he said, crying. "Please."

The sight of the bleeding, blubbering man unnerved Penny.

"How old are you?" she asked.

"Sixty-six," he said, sobbing.

"Did you *really* just want to scare Belon?"

"It's the God's honest truth. He was like my son, ya

know. I picked him up when he was just a little tyke. Streets of St. Louis. You should have seen him then—all rough an' tumble. He was like my son. "

"He told me that he didn't want to end up like you."

"I know he didn't always respect me. Hey, I'm an ordinary Joe. Not much education. No family. But he was like one of my own. I loved him 'til the end, I'm telling you. I'd never hurt him."

"Take your clothes off."

"What?!"

"Undress!"

"I don't really want to."

"Undress or I'll blow your fucking head off!"

There were streaks of blood all over his naked body. He was frightened, she could tell.

"Ok, I've seen enough. Put your clothes on."

She cleaned him up, tending to his wound.

"Was Belon a good kisser?" he suddenly said.

"You know, you're a brazen asshole. Maybe that's why you run a circus."

Penny pulled out a cigarette from her purse and blew a lazy ring of smoke into the air. "I actually don't mind, though. Whatever gets you through life, I suppose. Anyway, as far as your silly question is concerned, yes, he was a pretty good kisser. Sometimes he'd bite, though."

The impresario contemplated for a minute and cleared his throat. "I'll bet he wasn't as good as me." He kissed her on the mouth, passionately and forcefully. Penny's body jolted but she did not resist.

☮

The circus left San Francisco shortly thereafter. There was some discussion about reopening in N.Y. but it never happened—Belon's death cast a pall over the circus; it now had a wicked reputation, one that was so widely known that North America seemed unmercifully small.

In Paris it was another story. The public there had read in carefully-timed news releases orchestrated by McDuff about this high-wire performer, Penny was her name. *Escape to the land of the fairy tale!* it was written in the release. So large crowds gathered beneath scorching suns. Many patrons waited for hours. This was the *World's Biggest Circus* after all. A circus like no other.

SLEEPLESS

WHEN MY GRANDPA was sixty-eight, he fell down the stairs at our house and hit the back of his head. I was only eleven at the time but I remember the incident well. I was playing computer games in my room when I heard a few loud thuds following by groaning. There he lay, crumpled up near the bottom of the staircase, spots of blood dotting the carpet.

"Call Nana," he whispered feebly.

My grandmother was in the bathroom and came out with cream all over her face. "Oh my ..." she exclaimed when she saw her husband. I'm pretty sure her next word was 'God' but it never came out—she promptly fainted.

When the ambulance came, they took both Nana and Papa away on stretchers. Nana only got cream into her eyes and had to have them washed out but Papa was far worse off. He had a broken leg, two cracked ribs, a deflated lung and a concussion.

I visited him every day, as did my parents, who felt terrible because the carpeting on the stairs hadn't been tacked down properly when he slipped. They blamed themselves for the accident and tried to make it up by catering to his every need. I remember my mom and Nana were in the kitchen all the time. Mom was a great baker—banana bread, apple pie, chocolate chip cookies, carrot cake — and Nana was really good at the more substantial stuff, soups and stews mostly.

At the hospital, I would hold his hand and tell him that birds sing after a storm and that people can hold onto that thought during the worst times because they too can be singing again. I got it from a poetry book we were studying at school and Papa loved to hear me say it.

"I like singing," he said.

"I know, I hear you all the time. Sometimes you hum."

"Yes, sometimes I do hum, especially when I don't know the words."

After the hospital, he was sent to a rehab centre where they taught him to use his leg again and to walk properly. He was there even longer than in the hospital and I remember that I didn't visit as often because the rehab centre was quite far away from where I lived and mom wanted me to do my homework after school. That was ok because by the time he was in there, I already knew that he'd be fine again. Things were on the mend.

And in time he was fine. After two months in the hospital and another three at the rehab centre, Papa went back to his own house. He was almost like the old Papa I used to know. The only thing different about him is that he would sometimes get a bit depressed. That was very different from how he used to be before the accident, when he was always happy. But Dad said that was understandable because of all that he had been through, but I always knew that something else was the matter. So one day I asked him. Papa stared at me blankly for a moment and then said: "I can't sleep properly, my little lemon cup." I liked it when he called me his *little lemon cup*. "It's our secret, okay?" I nodded and hugged him because having a secret with Papa made me feel close to him.

One day they took Papa back to the hospital. I was afraid when I saw him because he had all these wires hooked up. They came from his head and his chest and even his forefinger and he looked like an alien. Now he was back where he started and I couldn't understand how that had happened.

"It's my sleep, little lemon cup." I understood but felt a bit disappointed that our secret was out ... now all the doctors in the hospital knew.

He wasn't in the part of the hospital where he had once been, that much I knew. There were no nurses running around and nobody was groaning or screaming. I read the sign in the ward and it said: 'SLEEP DISORDERS CLINIC.'

While I understood that Papa was back in the hospital because of a sleep problem, I didn't really and truly get it. I loved sleeping. I could sleep all day long if only Mom had let me. Every morning when she came to wake me to get ready to go to school, I'd roll over and tell her that I wanted to sleep five more minutes. Weekends were best because I could always sleep late.

I didn't dare touch all the wires but wondered how anyone could sleep with all of them hooked up to your body anyway. They were criss-crossed and all tangled up and looked like slippery, thin-coloured snakes crawling up his body. Before I left I told Papa to have good dreams but I thought it was more likely that he might have nightmares.

I tried to find out what was wrong with Papa but no one in my family would tell me. So one Saturday I rode my bike over to Nana and Papa's to get some answers. I knew it would be best to talk to Nana alone so I told Papa, who was now back from the hospital, that I had forgotten to get some treats for Maddox, our dog. I knew that he would volunteer to drive over to the mall and pick some up for me.

"They're the organic ones," I reminded him as I saw him to the door. "They smell exactly like oatmeal raisin cookies."

"Can you eat them?" he asked me.

"Yes."

"Then maybe I'll just buy human oatmeal raisin cookies. We can munch on them ourselves and I'm sure Maddox won't mind."

"Papa!"

When he left, I had real oatmeal raisin cookies with milk, the very kind Papa had just joked about. I especially liked to see the cookies crumble and sink to the bottom of the glass, where I would fish them out with a long spoon. Nice and soggy.

I liked visiting with my grandparents because they talked to me like I was an adult. Much more so than my parents; to them, I was always their *little baby girl*. Nana was chopping onions for some tomato sauce she was making when her eyes became all teary.

"Don't worry, Nana, I'll take over," I said, but she told me the knife was too sharp. She gave me a long wooden spoon and let me mix the ingredients that were already simmering in a pot on the stove.

"How's Papa?" I said.

"Getting better every day."

"What about his sleep?" The words came out, just like that.

Nana stopped chopping and looked straight at me. I always liked that because I knew she was paying attention to what I was saying and ready to tell me something.

"Well, Wendy, since the accident, your Papa has had a hard time sleeping. When he fell and hit his head on the stairs, something happened to him."

I still didn't get it. I understood all the words but together they didn't make much sense. How could anyone have a hard time sleeping?

"The doctors think that when he got hit, things moved around in his head. Shaken up. They say that the sleep centre in his brain was damaged."

I went back to mixing the ingredients. I stirred hard and wished Nana had a nickname for me like Papa did, but she always just called me Wendy.

Over the next few years I saw less of my grandparents; mostly when I did it was during holidays—Christmas,

Thanksgiving. It's not that I didn't think of them, it's just that other things infiltrated my life—high school, best girl-friends, getting my eyebrows tinted (it was like, so awesome), music, parties and of course, boys.

When I did see my grandparents, they seemed just fine to me. Of course I noticed they were getting older, their grey hair was turning silver, almost white. But that was all. I really completely forgot about Papa's sleep problem, mostly because no one ever talked about it and also because there never seemed to be anything wrong with him. Whenever the holidays rolled around, Papa seemed in great spirits, laughing and telling jokes, just like he had always done.

All that changed one day. I had recently turned seventeen when I read the following article in the local newspaper:

> The only indication that Harold Morgan has not slept a wink in the past four years are the dark circles under his perpetually reddened eyes. Aside from that, Mr. Morgan gives all indications of being a perfectly healthy man of seventy-two. His dilemma started when he fell down a flight of stairs and suffered a second degree concussion.
>
> 'It was quite a fall,' Morgan recalls. 'Even broke my glasses.'
>
> Morgan has been the subject of numerous sleep tests and the ongoing medical evidence would suggest that he has lost all ability to actually fall asleep. Although doctors do not have an easy answer for it, the accident somehow irreparably shattered the sleep centres in his brain. Although

he can get into a highly relaxed, immobilized state when he tries to sleep, EEG's show that his brain is still wide awake.

Morgan has tried progressive body relaxation, mindfulness meditation, sleep tapes, sleeping pills, melatonin, SSRI's, chronotherapy (involves progressively delaying his bedtime to later hours, thus resetting his biological clock), hypnotherapy, bright lights (used to treat SAD patients), acupuncture, electro-shock therapy, exercise, modifying his sleep environment (he and his wife now have separate twin beds), changing his diet, abstaining from alcohol and caffeine, and even eating an apple every morning at seven AM while staring at a photo of the Arc de Triomphe.

'Someone told me about Alexander Dumas, the author of *The Count of Monte Cristo*,' says Morgan. 'He suffered from insomnia and his doctor ordered him to eat an apple every morning under the Arc. I knew it was a long shot but I thought what the heck, why not give it a try — it actually worked for Dumas.'

Doctors are perplexed at how a man with no ability to sleep can function. Although it is not known with any certainty why man must sleep, it has long been thought that deep sleep is necessary for the body to repair itself. Not so in Morgan's case; he is a man whose organs and functions remain intact and vital.

'He's a medical wonder,' says his treating

physician Dr. Stanley S. Richards. 'My only theory is that his body has adapted to his inability to sleep. Humans have changed through evolution; who knows, we may be witness to the very first time a human morphs from a creature who must sleep to one who needs no sleep at all. Evolution in the making.'

What does a man who is awake twenty-four hours a day do at night, when most of the world is fast asleep? 'There's so much to do,' says Morgan. 'There are books to read and music to listen to — I'll never in my lifetime finish reading or listening to all that I want. If I really feel bored, I can go to an all-night bingo parlour — I've made some good friends there. I can stare at pictures of my beautiful grandchildren all day and night, instead of only during the daylight hours. I like to spend time in the kitchen, preparing dishes for family and friends ... that's a source of joy for me. I'm pretty good at making cherry pies and banana bread, rice pudding, desserts mostly. What else? Well, sometimes I just like snuggling next to my wife, listening to her sleep and watching over her. And if the weather's nice and I feel like walking, I'll go around the neighbourhood. I like to think of myself as the guardian of the night.'

His wife of forty-nine years, Edna Morgan, says that her husband is a treasure. 'When this first happened, I thought it was a tragedy. I used to cry all the time, sometimes for me, mostly for Harold. But he's handled it so well, I couldn't possibly feel any sadness. He inspired me before the accident and even moreso after. I don't know what I'd do without him.'

Dr. Richards comments that Morgan's body temperature is often abnormally low. 'We don't really understand why.'

Only periodically does Morgan agree to be tested by medical experts, many who are from various parts of the globe. 'I have a life to live, he says. 'I can't be holed up in doctors' offices and hospitals, being a guinea pig.'

After I finished the article I cried my eyes out. It seemed that for many days following, I continued to cry; I'd just burst out in tears every time I thought of my Papa. I don't even know why I was crying, only that I was. All sorts of emotions welled up in me but the strongest by far was one of love—I just loved Papa so much.

From that moment on, I made it a point to visit with Nana and Papa, even if it meant curtailing my social activities. I never mentioned the article nor did they. I often wondered why Papa had agreed to being featured in it, what his motivation was to allow himself to be revealed in such a manner. Knowing Papa as I did, those motivations were selfless, meant to help others. As for my parents, they too never brought up the issue of the newspaper article, although I was pretty sure they were aware of it ... my dad read the newspaper every single day.

About a year after the article appeared, Papa died. The doctors said the cause was a massive heart attack. I had noticed during my last few visits that he seemed particularly fatigued, much more than usual. I saw that he sometimes steadied himself against a counter, a table, the fridge ... anything he could find really. Almost like he was dizzy. Sometimes I even saw him use a cane when he was outside. A cane! Papa was so proud of his ability to be fully mobile without any aids that it was almost a sacrilege to him. And then there were his afternoon rests, which stretched into hours and hours. Moreover, the colour in his face had drained and his skin looked pasty, sickly.

When Mom told me that he had died, I cried and cried. It seemed like the tears would never stop. But then suddenly one day they did. Just like that. It was the strangest thing. It would be too awful to say that I felt happy about Papa's death, yet that's how I felt. Happy for him. I thought about how his ordeal was now over; my Papa would no longer be the guardian of the night and that suited me all too well.

RITE OF PASSAGE

HE IS ON vacation at an all-inclusive resort in Jamaica, away from the forced daily grind of his life. He walks the perimeter of the pool. Tourists sun themselves in oversized blue lounge chairs, an army of hedonists. Couples abound, lathering lotion onto each other. He finds a chair near an elderly couple, removed from the vibrant crowds. Sedate old coots, this location will do just fine.

He sees a woman hand a digital camera to her partner. "My new screensaver," she says, posing strategically at the pool's edge, her bronzed head tossed back. In the water, Frisbees are tossed about, and people ride shotgun on each others' backs. A weathered-looking man wearing a straw hat and with a parakeet perched on his shoulder wanders about. "Ya picture with da bird," he says. "Only ten dollars U.S., mon. Bootiful memories of Jamaica."

It is oppressively hot and he can use a drink. There is a bar in the middle of the pool where people stand waist-deep, glasses in hand, and bounce to the beat of reggae sounds. He dare not wade out there ... he would rather go thirsty.

Gusts of strong wind rattle the pages of his book, making it impossible to read. He is not much of a swimmer, he knows, so slips into the water where it is only three feet deep. Beside him four children bat a sponge ball about with wooden paddles and a woman dips her baby backside down into the water, like she is anointing it.

He gets out of the water only to realize that a young couple now occupy the chairs next to him. They fawn over each other and speak in hushed tones in a secret language all their own. *Love*—it nauseates hum to the core; he prefers to go it alone.

He eats at the buffet that is replete with Jamaican food—curried goat, jerk chicken, beef, pork, salt fish and octopus. Fried foods—yams and plantains. There is also a section for the American palate—French fries, turkey with gravy, meat loaf, lasagna, Chicken Cacciatore, Hunter's Stew. If only he could find a tomato or cucumber, something light, salad would be best. He eats the assorted cheeses, at least there is that.

At the beach, he puts his towel down and slathers himself with sunscreen. Maybe here he can read in peace. He shields his eyes and looks up—the sun is burnt orange and yellow; it looks syrupy, like bits and bobs have broken off and are cascading down ... some, he is sure, are landing directly on his chest. He can barely breathe. *I am in hell*, he thinks.

A woman, soaking wet, comes in from the sea and places her towel close to his. She shakes her head vigorously, spraying him.

"Pardon-moi," she says, laughing. He says nothing, only offering a slight smile.

"Nous sommes des roommates," she says giggling, and

he realizes that she is adept at this type of thing, the art of the pickup. Two languages, hedging her bets. He tells her his name but he does this out of courtesy only. At first glance, she appears like all the others at the resort—overfed, unaware.

"Monique Proulx is my name," she says.

"There's a singer with the same name."

"There is?"

"I don't know," he replies. "Maybe. It's a good name for a singer." His feeble attempt at humour goes undetected, she does not laugh.

"Why are you here in Jamaica?" she asks.

He suspects this is her way of finding out whether he is alone.

"It's a good question," he says laconically. "I've been asking myself the same thing the past three days."

"So, what is your answer, monsieur?"

"To look into the dark void. To look but hopefully not to fall in."

She looks at him askew, as if he were speaking a foreign language. He can tell that she doesn't understand, which is not surprising—he himself has no clear idea what he meant. He feels embarrassed by his answer and excuses himself, saying he must meet his girlfriend.

At dinner that night, he tells the waiter that he has heard there is life in Kingston, a different kind of life. It is a remark borne of frustration and loneliness, the resort seems too sterile.

"Maybe so but I would not go there alone," he is told.

The comment is enough to spur him to act. At the front of the resort are taxis and he engages one driver. "Kingston," he says with authority.

"Where exactly, mon?"

"Downtown Kingston."

"No, mon. Et is not for you."

"Just do what I say."

The drive takes him through the countryside past rows of dilapidated, clapboard shacks. Laundry flaps in the breeze and he realizes that people actually live in these miserable places. Where well-heeled tourists filled his sightline, now he sees the bare minimum for human existence. Broken, makeshift shelters without front doors. Hand pumps for water. The landscape is dotted with skinny goats, horses and chickens. But he looks on neutrally, as if it is a shame, but not his concern. He is, however, glad to be out of Shangri-la, of that he is certain.

The driver honks at what looks like a pack of large rats blocking the highway. They are the size of cats, which unnerves him, the passenger.

"Mongoose," the driver says. "Brought here from dem India country to get rid of da rats and now dey is pests demselves—eat all dem beautiful birds. And love dem mangoes and bananas, eat dem all."

"Great. A history lesson."

The rest of the ride continues in silence for which he is happy. The last thing he wants is small talk. In Kingston, the driver asks him where he wants to be let off.

"I don't know ... a bar?"

They stop in front of an industrial-looking building with corrugated iron covering the windows. COOL RUN-

NIN'S, the painted white letters read. A queue of people has formed outside.

"Fifty-seven dollars U.S.," the driver says. "Cash only."

Cash? Christ! It only now occurs to him that he hadn't thought of the money he would need for this trip. He searches his wallet—seventy-seven dollars plus his credit card. He hands the driver sixty-two, keeping the rest for a drink. The credit card he will use for the ride back. Hopefully a different driver will take it.

Stares follow him as he takes his place in line. "White boy don't belong here," the black man in front turns to tell him.

"Just here for a drink," he says. "Can't take the resort. Full of tourists, full of money." He immediately regrets having said that—he himself is a white man in an expensive resort ... probably not so smart.

He hands the incredulous doorman five dollars and is let in. Now he is down to ten dollars. No way will he use his credit card in a place like this. The joint is a dump, the worst he has ever been in. It reeks of vomit, cheap wine, and weed. The floorboards creak under his weight. People stand around talking in groups, drinking and smoking. He hears laughter and the clacking of pool balls. He is jostled, buffeted by the flow of the crowds, but manages to break free and takes a seat in the darkest area of the club, near the stage.

"Ya here for da dance class, boy," someone says.

He waits for something to happen—a show to start or a waiter to take his order—but nothing does. In a strange way, he is grateful for it, that he can exist in oblivion. But he begins to wonder why he is in this place. Not *this place* but rather Jamaica. He needed to get away from his life in Montreal to be certain, his life as a suit in the downtown business core, but he could have gone to Paris, or London, anywhere there is culture, intellect.

Maybe I have come here to die. Maybe not to die literally (although that is a possibility) but to die inside. To completely fall apart. So that he could start over again. With every ending there is a beginning. Something new. He has been feeling inert for a long time now, even depressed. Like his soul has been deadened. Apathy, anxiety, despair, and loneliness have been his constant companions. He is not sure why he has been feeling this way but puts it down to his job. Working for a large company has its perks, the money and toys, a nice car, a fancy condo, but he has had to sell his soul. Or so it seems.

What then is left of me? He has spent long hours in the office, often working weekends and evenings. And to what end? He has few friends, hasn't had a girlfriend in a long time, and moreover, hasn't had the time to enjoy the things he could buy. He has never once gone into the sauna in his condo building, never once dipped his toes in the swimming pool, never lifted a single weight in the gym. And although he loves reading, he hasn't read a book in a long time. At least his parents are happy for his success. He is a good son, they have told him many times … he reflects upon that.

So why not Paris? he asks himself yet again. *Yes, why not?* He already speaks the language. He gives his head a shake and understands that coming to Jamaica may simply be the denouement of his disintegration. There is no other answer.

The stage is suddenly lit by yellow and magenta spotlights and all at once he becomes a prop on it. Hustled by four men and made to sit on a stool. He attempts to leave but is restrained. His heart though is racing, feeling as if it will explode from his chest cavity and suffocate him.

"I'm not looking for trouble. I just came to relax," he tells the men.

"We want you to relax, mon," one says.

Another interjects: "Stage fright? Don't worry, mon. Now you are an actor and it is natural to be afraid. You are trying something new, a rite of passage, mon."

Throbbing music, sounding angry and spiteful, resonates in his ears and from the corner of his eye he sees a woman saunter onto the stage. By all appearances a woman ... hair, makeup, dress. But she is far too large, too muscular. Some sort of freak of nature is what she really is. When she whispers to him 'enjoy yourself,' it is with a robust, mannish voice. He swoons with fear, his head lolling back as if it is going to roll from his shoulders.

"Please," he says in a panic, and it is all he has left, to beg—nothing in his life has prepared him for this moment. The freak sidles up to him, gyrating in time to the music, and sits on his lap.

"Kees her, kees her," he hears disembodied voices in the audience yell out. His world narrows and all he sees are the pouting lips. Prodded by the men who hold him, he leans forward and purses his own lips.

"Yeah mon! Yeah mon!"

The woman grinds her thick thighs against his and he wants to wretch. She sways back and forth violently and he closes his eyes to mute the anxiety. Nimble fingers caress his scalp and teeth bite into the side of his neck. After a time, she is worn out, he can see that. She breathes heavily, the Adam's apple rising. Perspiration dots her frantic face; it glistens the short hairs that adorn the upper lip.

He is bodily lifted up and escorted out the back of the club, his shoes scraping the floorboards as he goes. Relieved, he wants to run but is weak on his feet, and feels like collapsing onto the ground. From behind, someone places something onto his temple. The coldness of metal against warm flesh.

"No joke, mon. Gimme what you have."

His hands trembling, he removes a thin wallet from his back pocket.

"Ten bucks, mon? Ten lousy bucks?" The lunatic holds up the ATM and Visa cards. "We will drive to da bank ... no games and no one gets hurt, my friend. And we are friends, after all."

The bank machine applies a six dollar service charge on his five-hundred dollar withdrawal. "Rip-off," he tells the gunman, trying to engage in friendly banter; he thinks it will stand him in good stead.

"No problem, mon. You can afford it. Fancy white boy."

He hands over the money and his cards and writes down his pin number on a slip of paper. The assailant walks away whistling and slides into a beat-up Chevy.

The thought crosses his mind that the worst is over, that he is still alive. But even that is no certainty, not in this foreign land. He starts to walk but soon sits down at a curbside and cries. He realizes his pants are wet, he has peed into them. Passers-by ogle him, a white person in their milieu, but they take no liberties, his tears acting as a buffer.

He glances at his watch, it is just after midnight. He ponders what to do next. Somehow, amidst the frayed electrons that pummel his brain, a reasoned thought arises— he must look for a phone booth. *Do they still exist?* He left his cell back at the resort and has no choice. He gets to his feet and begins to put one foot in front of the other. Walks by a man urinating against a wall and then past an erotic bookstore. He finds a solitary payphone against a pole. It is rife with dirt but he doesn't care.

"Operator, operator, I've been mugged. Please call the Gran Bahia Hotel for me. I beg of you, I have no money, no credit cards."

"You should make a report to the police, sir." He hears a clicking noise of the tongue coming from the faceless person, like he is being scolded.

"You don't understand. I am all alone. Please operator, the Gran Bahia in Runaway Bay."

It is soon arranged. He is driven back to the Gran Bahia in a taxi paid for by the resort, and collapses theatrically on a couch in the lobby.

"You have no idea," he tells the security staff who come out to meet him. The police are called. Then the bank. He takes to his bed and pulls the covers up to his chin. It is 4:20 am and he is wide awake, exhausted but alert. And most importantly, alive. He is perplexed how the people who assaulted him can be so callous, so insensitive. Gradually his mind grows calm and the saving grace of sleep overtakes him.

The next day he is on a plane to Montreal. At the airport there, he is greeted by the one friend he has left, an old grade-school school buddy, who has come to drive him home.

"How was your trip?"

He lets out a sigh and frowns. "I don't know. I've been through a bunch of shit but as they say in Jamaica, *I lost da fear, mon.* At least some."

"That sounds good. Positive."

"Maybe. But I also think I might have lost a little bit of myself there. It's almost like I need to change, I guess."

"I think you had already lost some of yourself here in Montreal, before you left," his friend tells him. "You were already another person—I hardly ever saw you."

"I know, I've been working a lot."

"I was going to say, I hardly ever saw you *smile*. You've lost a lot of joy, that's what I think."

"You're right. I have. But I couldn't help it. I just couldn't."

"Anyway, you know, sometimes that's not a bad thing, losing yourself. Sometimes it signals that it's time for a change. That parts need to die. What do you think, huh?"

"Maybe," he says. "I was thinking that myself. Okay, so any suggestions on how to change things then?"

"Another trip."

"What?"

"Sure, I'll go with you this time. As the song says— *first, we'll take Manhattan, then we'll take Berlin.*"

At last he laughs. "Manhattan and Berlin. Sounds appealing. We'll see, though," he says. "We'll see. But you know how hard it is for me to change. You've known me a long time."

"That's true. Change comes slowly to you, my friend. But think about Mr. Cohen's lyrics. And you've got all this vacation time left."

And as he leans his head against the car's pane of glass, he realizes that sand from the beach grates in his shoes.

A week later, while crossing a busy street in Montreal, he is hit by a car. He was jaywalking, not paying attention, talking on his phone. In the hospital, he is given the bad news —his left leg is broken in two places. Surgery follows; now he is full of pins and screws.

His friend visits. "I can't believe it," he says. "You were on your phone when you got whacked by a car?"

"Not just any car though. A BMW X5."

"Get real!"

"Hey, it's $600,000. I guess if I'm going to get hit by any car, that's about the best I can do. Anyway, I was on the phone, I'll admit it. I was talking to a client."

"Christ. I'm worried about you, you don't know how to stop."

"I can take care of myself."

"Yeah, right. And I'm Batman." His friend taps him gently on the forehead. "Look, I'll come by in the next few days to check up. I'll bring some good food. And we'll make a plan to get away. In the meantime, rest. And remember, first Manhattan, then we take Berlin."

Later that same day, he is visited by his boss, who carries a large bouquet of very expensive flowers—lilies and peonies.

"Those are beautiful. Thank you."

"Sophie chose them; she's concerned. Of course about your health but also about the account you were working on for her. Actually, we're both concerned."

The boss shakes his head and pushes his glasses further up the bridge of his nose. "I don't really know what we're going to do now," he says. "The account you were working on will go down the drain. You've spent so much time and energy on it. And you're really the only one who can do it."

"As soon as I get out of here, sir, I'll start on it again. Just give me a few days. I'll get out sooner than you think."

"You sure?"

"Yes. Absolutely."

He lobbies the doctors for an early discharge. "I'm better off at home," he tells them. "I'll just bring in some nursing care."

When his friend visits him in the hospital, carrying a basket of fruit and brochures about Manhattan and Berlin, he is not there.

"Discharged," the nurse says.

"Discharged? But he just had surgery. How can that be?"

The nurse shrugs. "Not my decision," she says. "Speak to the doctors."

He hands over the basket of fruit. "Here, for you," he says.

⚬⚬

At his home, the IT department of his company are hard at work, setting up a computer. He already has a company phone. Working from home, it is all the rage in the corporate world. Now he is all set.

He doesn't miss a beat, working long hours. Of course he is in pain and extremely uncomfortable, but he soldiers on—he has lots to assist him, a morphine drip administered by a homecare nurse, Percocet that he eats like candy.

Sometimes he feels delirious, his head swoons, his forehead breaks into cold sweats. He resists the urge to lie down, knowing that if he does, he will waste precious working hours. Similarly, he ignores his friend's calls, which go straight to voice mail—there is simply too much to do. But after many weeks, it is all over. The project has been completed. Now he has been summoned back to the office.

"You went over and above the call of duty," his beaming boss says, sitting behind his oak desk. Sophie stands next to him. She too is all smiles.

"The work is so good," she tells him.

He looks at her through bleary eyes. She is an older woman, in her late fifties, and has been with the company over 25 years. Worked her way up from a secretarial position and is now high in the pecking order. The boss's favourite. But time has not been kind, her hair is white, her face is lined. Deep lines. Some emanate down from the corners of her mouth and it gives her the appearance of a marionette, at least to him it does … the man standing there gingerly on crutches. The man who is ashen-faced.

"We were talking it over," the boss says, rubbing his hands gleefully, "and have come to the conclusion that you will take a vacation on us. Company expense account. Anywhere you like. What do you say?"

"How about Greece?" Sophie says. "I went there as a child. Rome. The Parthenon."

"Italy is very nice this time of year," the boss says, looking knowingly at Sophie and smiling. "You should go to Italy. The Amalfi Coast."

"Well really, it's your decision," Sophie says.

The patient, *yes, the patient, for he is still on pain medication and taking physical therapy when not working*, takes a deep breath. "Now that I think of it," he says, "there is one place I wouldn't mind going."

"Just name it," the boss says, crossing his arms. "I'm ready to send you anywhere. You deserve everything."

I deserve nothing, he thinks. But he doesn't say that. Instead, he whispers:

"I was thinking of Jamaica."

EARTH DAY

JEREMY WHITELY WASN'T planning on beheading the old woman but his words were enough to cause her to keel over. "Go ahead, I dare you," he said in a staccato fashion. "I don't want that rag and besides, you've killed trees to make it."

With one last piercing look, Jeremy left the old woman standing on the steps leading to his house, and started up on his bike. He was unaware of the effect he had on her until he returned home from work later in the evening and saw the yellow police tape wrapped like a Xmas present around the front of his house.

In between, his day had been like any other. His work as a bike courier took him into the bowels of downtown Toronto where he rode the wrong way on streets, through red lights, up on sidewalks and down stairs, causing terrified pedestrians to jump out of the way. Along the way, he managed to hurl a basket-full of insults to car owners: "Think about the environment! Up your ass with hydro-carbons! Looks like you want to get your mirror broken driving in my lane!"

But it wasn't only motorists who were the recipients of Jeremy's wrath. To a man talking on his cell: "Brain cancer, buddy. Right where you're holding that phone." To a pack of vagrants hovering above a grate: "Millionaire's row, boys." To a kid asking for a handout: "Get a job." To an overweight woman: "Gym time, lady."

Carrying x-rays, architectural drawings, legal documents and anything else that fit into his tattered shoulder bag, Jeremy zipped around the city with one purpose in mind—get the stuff delivered as quickly as possible. He had a general disdain for anyone other than his fellow messengers and in particular for business types, whom he saw as corporate drones, lacking in imagination, a little too proud of the drab grey and blue suits they wore like badges of honour. He would stand in the elevators next to the suits, adorned with his ear and lip rings and various tattoos, sweaty and smelly, a slight smile curling the sides of his mouth. If he felt particularly disdainful that day, he would open his mouth and pretend to yawn, so that the silver bauble sitting in the middle of his tongue was fully visible.

It didn't matter that he despised the very people who utilized his services; he was anti-corporate and anti-establishment. He thought himself an artist in the way he lived his life, a Chagall, a Picasso, full of passion, colour, and most of all free. Free to do as he pleased, an entrepreneur on a ten-speed, not tied to a corporation where he was forced to sell his soul for money. He was poor and that was fine; it was a small price to pay for his independence. So if he grabbed a fistful of candy from a receptionist's desk, gave someone the finger, or caused pedestrians to scatter, these were just splashes of bold colours that he was adding to the tapestry of his exciting life.

It hadn't always been that way. In fact, for a number of years, Jeremy Whitley had been one of those business types that he so disliked. With a degree in Economics and a rising star in the Royal Bank's Management Training Program, he was destined for great things, a powerhouse in the corporate world. But he lost it all when he was charged with pilfering change from the teller's till. Why he did it, Jeremy could not say with any certainty—impulse perhaps more than anything. It was just a wee bit of loose cash to buy a coffee, go to the movies. *My petty cash*, as Jeremy liked telling himself. The bank made millions upon millions, what was a few lost dollars to them? But the charge of 'two hundred and under' left him on probation for two years.

Ash and smoke darkened his star and made him unemployable in the world he had known, a virtual pariah. And although Jeremy fully acknowledged his guilt, he felt the bank could have handled it differently, internally. In fact, he offered to pay the money back and resign. He begged for leniency, hoping to erase the matter from his life. Instead, the bank called the police which in turn led to the charges. From that moment on, with a record hovering like a black cloud, Jeremy was reborn into an angry young man with spiky hair and an attitude. He hung out with artists, bike couriers, musicians, anyone who didn't abide by society's rules. He spoke of making the world a little bit better and made sure no one in his circle ever talked about ridiculous things like stock prices, mutual funds, and bottom lines.

But everything changed the day he yelled at the old woman who was delivering the local neighbourhood paper. He was met on the sidewalk by a phalanx of blue-uniformed police officers.

"What's your business here?" he was asked as he pulled up on his 2-wheeled limousine.

"What am *I* doing here?" he said. "What are *you* doing here?"

A man with a handlebar moustache and wearing a drab grey suit stepped forward: "Listen Mohawk Boy, don't give us your attitude. *We'll* be asking the questions, not you. Speak only when you're spoken to." He was short and rotund, his clothes almost busting at the seams, in sharp contrast to Jeremy, who was pencil-thin and tall at six foot two inches. Although Jeremy normally flouted any authority, he could sense this guy wasn't to be messed with. There was also the matter of the imposing black-holstered gun that was strapped to the man's belt.

"My name's Detective Peter Jackson. Do you live here?"

"Peter Jackson? Isn't that a cigarette brand?" Jeremy said.

"You think you're funny?" The detective stood on his toes and moved his face close to Jeremy's.

"No, sir," Jeremy said. His heart was thumping.

"Good." Jackson turned to smile at his colleagues.

"So I live here," Jeremy said.

"Who else lives here?"

"There's four others. We're all bike couriers."

"Where are they?"

"I don't know. Maybe still working. Maybe with friends."

"I'll need all their names."

It was at that point that Jeremy noticed the white sheet draped over the steps of his house. It was obvious there was a body underneath.

"Who's that?"

"We were hoping you could tell us," Jackson said, leading Jeremy by the arm up the steps, and pulling the sheet up.

"I know her," Jeremy said. He had never seen a dead body before and the sight unnerved him; the woman's face was pasty, devoid of all colour. It made him want to wretch but he held it in. Acid soured his lungs.

"I mean, I don't *reeeally* know her," he said, his eyes misty. "She's just the old lady who delivers the paper in the neighbourhood. Community newspaper. It's a rag if you ask me."

"Have some respect, ok?"

Jeremy nodded.

"One of your neighbours saw you having a confrontation with her this morning," Jackson said.

"I never saw her before today and so just told her I didn't want the paper. That's all."

"Did you push her?"

"What? No. No, definitely not," Jeremy said, his back up.

"Did you see her fall?"

"What? No. Definitely not. What happened to her anyway?"

"I ask the questions," Jackson said, drawing his eyebrows together into a scowl.

Jeremy removed his well-worn bike gloves. He looked at the detective and got the distinct impression that the latter considered him a suspect. He never trusted the police, and now remembered why. The woman must have had a heart attack—what did that have to do with him?

"Can I have a look in the house?" Jackson asked.

"No. What for?" Suddenly Jeremy got his dander back.

Jackson pulled out a cigarette and blew a smoke ring. "You have nothing to hide, right?"

"I know my rights. Do you have a warrant?"

Jackson turned to his colleagues. "The boy's been watching those cop shows—*CSI* and *Law & Order*." His remark elicited laughter but Jeremy remained stone-faced.

"Some hash is in plain sight," Jackson said, pointing to the window.

"There's no hash and even if there was, you couldn't possibly see it through the curtains."

"X-ray vision," Jackson said, forcing Jeremy's arm behind his back.

"Ow, you fucker."

"Look, I don't like you, Mohawk Boy, and I don't care what you think. So you're going to open the front door voluntarily like a good boy and I'm going to look in your place."

Jeremy was right—there was no hash. But Jackson found a bag of Mexican Gold sitting in plain view in the living room and Jeremy was quickly handcuffed and stuffed into a police car. "Police brutality!" he yelled out the window to a passer-by. "They hit me! Get your cell out and take a picture." He turned away and smacked himself in the eye, reddening it. "See, right here," he said, pointing to his eye.

The passer-by continued walking.

"Since the first Earth Day on April 22, 1970," Jeremy screamed, now to no one in particular, "we've lost more than one billion acres of forest! It's an apocalypse. And that old woman was part of the problem! A big part of the problem!"

Mohawk Boy was taken to a holding cell downtown, where his cellmate was 'Ice,' a full-patch member of a bike gang called The Esperantos. Jeremy thought he looked like a refugee from the 70's ... long black hair parted down the middle, mutton chops, and a big droopy Fu Manchu moustache.

Ice showed Jeremy his many tattoos, including a shiny Harley-Davidson etched between his shoulder blades, and on his leg, a scantily-clad woman slinking down a strip pole. For his part, Jeremy told Ice about the old woman who died on his doorstep.

"It's not like I had anything to do with it," he said. "So what do they do? They take my dope, all but accuse me of killing the old hag, and throw me into a cell."

Ice sniffed loudly and wiped away the snot that was running down his nose into his 'stash. He stared at Jeremy without blinking. "Look, let me tell you something," he said. "You'd better start to understand who in this life is your friend and who is your enemy. When you find that out, your life becomes a lot easier. And guess what? Most people won't turn out to be your friend. Most people are scum. The kind of stuff you scrape off the soles of your shoes. Bottom feeders. The only people you can trust are people like me and my kind."

Ice went on for a full three minutes lecturing Jeremy about how dreadful most everyone was and toward the end of his rant, he was vibrating like an outboard motor; snot and saliva dotting his face.

The longer Ice spoke, the more Jeremy liked Ice. It seemed they had a lot in common, like their general disdain for people.

"You know, Ice, when I was working for the bank, I had a pretty good deal. The money was fine and there was a lot more of it if only I had stayed with the program. Let me tell you, at the top of the heap are all the senior execs, who line their pockets with big dineros. And I was being groomed to be one of them."

"But like you said, you took that small amount of change."

"Yah, I did. You know why? I guess it's because I couldn't stand my co-workers. Yah, maybe that's why, now that I really think of it. It's almost like I sabotaged my own career. I'd go into the lunchroom every day and listen to the old hens prattle on about their pathetic families, how they thought their problems were so important. And the romance books they read!" Jeremy stuck his forefinger down his throat. "They were so boring, I could have died. I couldn't imagine spending my whole life surrounded by people like that."

"Maybe though when you worked your way up the corporate ladder, you would have been surrounded by a different kind of people."

"And that's the point!" Jeremy shouted, throwing his arms apart for emphasis. "Up at head office are all the execs. And they only care about one thing—earning as much money as possible. They step on other people to get to the top. They're sociopaths, they just don't care. And I just couldn't see myself living that way. It would have killed me."

"But now you have nothing."

"That's not true, Ice. I have my friends, that's really important."

"What about your family?"

"Estranged. As soon as they saw that I had been booted from the bank and took on a new lifestyle, they didn't want to have anything to do with me."

"So your friends is your family."

"Yup."

"That's like me," Ice said. "All my biker friends, that's all the family I have."

Jeremy and Ice sat in quiet contemplation for a few minutes.

"What happened to your eye?" Ice said, breaking the silence. "Looks all red, like ya got punched."

"Yah, police hit me when they arrested me."

"Fuckin' bastards. I hate the coppers. They make my life difficult."

"Me too."

Three hours later, Jeremy was let out, a strict warning that he stay in town still ringing in his ears, his court date for possession of drugs still pending. If he was embittered before the episode, Jeremy was positively spinning with venom after.

As he set out for work the next morning, Jeremy was very ornery. On his way downtown, he passed an old woman shaking out a mop on her porch and Jeremy threw the pit of his peach at her. "Stop polluting!" he yelled. "And go get a job!" It was no better downtown. "You're ugly!" he said to a prostitute standing at the corner of Jarvis and Adelaide as he cycled by.

"You too," came back the snappy retort, catching Jeremy off-guard.

"I call 'em like I see 'em, lady."

All day Jeremy's worries continued to grow, and he became downright nervous, stopping a number of times during his deliveries to smoke cigarettes, unusual for him since he normally only smoked dope. The events of the previous day were unnerving to be certain but when he put it in perspective, he had no reason to fret—he had nothing to do with the old woman's demise and certainly from a legal perspective, he was in the clear. And the amount of marijuana taken from his house was actually not that much; he and his roomies might get a few hundred dollar fine. Maybe. No, something else was on his mind and as the day wore on, it began to crystallize for him—someone was following him. Someone on a bike. But each time he turned around to face his follower, no one was there.

He decided he would flush the person out. So he threaded his way through the meandering streets of the downtown core and followed a narrow pedestrian dirt path into an alleyway that was home to heroin addicts and derelicts sleeping under cardboard boxes.

He chained his bike to an iron stairway and picked up a piece of pipe that lay on the ground. Then he hid in the back alcove of an abandoned plastics factory and waited.

It was late in the day and no one was around—the addicts usually came to life at night and the derelicts were out panhandling. He just had to be patient. Jeremy suddenly saw the giant oblique shadow of a bike's front tire coming his way. He held the pipe at the ready, slowly and silently pumping it a couple of times in his palm.

He could see the man now, walking alongside an old battered blue ten speed. As soon as he passed the alcove, Jeremy jumped out and whacked him in the back of the knees with the pipe. The man collapsed in a heap.

What freak of nature was this? The fallen man's heaving big belly strained at the skull and bones logo on his tight t-shirt. He was at least ten years older than Jeremy's twenty-seven years, maybe more. There was a Band-Aid perched under his blackened right eye and his face was rough and pockmarked, like the stretch of bad road Jeremy had to traverse every day on Adelaide, where the city road crews were tearing up the ground. His tartar beard was tied up with an elastic and Jeremy grabbed hold and tugged hard.

"You'd better have an answer, fat man!"

"I've just been asked to keep an eye on you," the man said.

"Really? Who sent you?!"

"Ice."

Jeremy let go of the man's beard. "You mean, the biker?"

"One in the same," the man said. "Can I get up now?"

Jeremy extended a hand. "Why is Ice watching me?"

"You should ask him yourself."

The two men set off for the biker's clubhouse on Eastern Avenue. Jeremy's riding companion—whose name was Duke—moved his thick legs so agonizingly slow that Jeremy had to shift down to a crawl to keep him in sight.

"How did you ever keep up with me throughout the day?" Jeremy asked.

"Oh, I lost you lots," Duke said, puffing. "But I figured you'd always show up at that Jet Fuel Café on Parliament, where all the couriers meet. And you did. Four times. So even if I lost you, I knew I'd see you there."

The clubhouse was fortified with bullet-proof windows and steel bars. Jeremy saw his reflection in a moving camera situated above the door.

Duke knocked hard on the door three times, hesitated and then knocked softly four times, in what was some sort of code.

Bond stuff, thought Jeremy.

The peephole went dark as someone looked through it. When Ice cracked the door open, he turned to someone inside: "Woo hoo. We've been graced with a bit of hippy-dippy stuff." He put an arm around Jeremy. "Good to see you, bro'," he said.

"You too."

Jeremy was introduced to the members on hand. There was Daddy, Skull, Chaz, Boxer, Heat, Smoke and Slasher. The only female there, a severe-looking woman with a buzz-cut, also had a nickname—*Teacher.* Jeremy had no interest in knowing what she taught.

Ice pulled Jeremy aside. "Sorry I put that tail on you buddy but I had to make sure you were who you said."

Jeremy looked around and saw that prominently displayed against a wall was a collection of guns and knives, a hand-held rocket launcher, grenades, as well as various other weapons that he couldn't identify. The entire display was adorned with a Confederate flag.

"Just memorabilia," Ice said. "Daddy and I like to collect war stuff." He walked over to the collection and pulled

a gun from the wooden rack. "See this. It's a Civil War re-
volver that they call a *Pepper Box*. I've used it to shoot beer
cans off people's heads."

Jeremy didn't know if he was lying or not but it didn't
matter. He was in a biker's house and that alone was worth
a story or two he could tell his friends. And Ice was a cool
guy, from what he could tell not dissimilar to him.

Ice put the gun on the table between them. "Look,
Mr. Jeremy, I brought you here because I want you to make
some deliveries for me. You told me in the cell that you don't
make too much good money driving your little bicycle
around. I'll pay you better, straight cash. Good bucks, my
friend. Dineros. Just liked you talked about. You'll be my
head office exec."

"I'm still a bike courier," Jeremy said. "That's my regular gig and I love it. But I can make deliveries for you at the
end of my day. Ok?"

"If you do everything I say, I'll throw in a little weed
now and then."

"How can I turn that down?"

It was the easiest money Jeremy had ever made. For the
most part, there was no problem making Ice's deliveries.
Sometimes though, the parcels were too large to take on
his bike, and Jeremy hopped in a cab. And there were
times the recipient at the other end gave him something to
bring back, sometimes not.

On one occasion, Jeremy was told to just make the drop
and not wait around. As he got off his bike and reached into

his backpack for the package, his hands turned crimson. The package was leaking and it wasn't Kool-Aid. He quickly deposited it onto the back porch of the house and took off down the road, finally stopping to wash his hands and pack in a park. A bloody secret coursing out from between the folds of the package but Jeremy didn't care. It wasn't his affair, and he didn't want to know about it. *None of my business*, he thought. *Just don't shoot the messenger.*

As the weeks passed, Jeremy found himself hanging out at the Esperantos' clubhouse. The people there weren't bad sorts, a little cruder than his own crowd, but that was alright ... he didn't have to marry them. And he found himself coming into Ice's confidence.

"I like you, Mr. Jeremy," Ice said, sitting on a black leather sofa. "If you ever think of leaving your little gang, you can maybe join up with us. Just like an intern, if you know what I mean. We're a relaxed group, as you can see. A social club."

Ice brought up the deliveries Jeremy was making, a subject the latter thought was off-limits.

"Sometimes I don't want to know," Jeremy said. "But I'd be lying if I said I wasn't a little curious, that's all."

"Drugs, mostly," Ice said, quite matter-of-factly. He knocked some hash from a pipe, filled it anew, and lit it. After a few drags, he passed it to Jeremy.

"I've got my own gig going," Jeremy said suddenly, inhaling deeply. "This is good shit, by the way."

"Ah, we only treat our guests with the most respect,"

Ice said, putting his feet up on a wooden coffee table. "So you've got your own gig, you said?"

"Well, yeah. Me and my friends, the guys I live with. We're the movers and shakers of our own little empire. Kind of a small one though, to be honest."

"Tell me more. Tell me more, my friend. I'm all ears."

So Jeremy, besotted with the good hash and feeling quite grand, revealed to Ice that he and his buddies had been running drugs, buying in moderate quantities and selling them. Mostly to other couriers, friends of friends, that sort of thing.

"If the police had any brains, they would have searched the whole house," he said. "They only found a small bag of Gold. It's just for personal use anyway. But the stuff we sell is hidden pretty good."

"Hey, a man after my own heart," Ice said. "Now I know why I like you."

"Yeah, but you know, our margins aren't so good. We're bike couriers and don't have all the right contacts. So like I said, the money isn't as good as it should be."

Ice leaned far forward. "I have contacts."

"That's what I was hoping you'd say. Music to my ears, Ice. One of the reasons I agreed to help you out."

"What's that saying," Ice said. "One hand butters the other ... something like that anyway."

"Yah, something like that," Jeremy said, laughing.

So the bicycle courier who made a vow never to talk about things like money and margins, was now up to his neck with them. He agreed to sell his drugs directly to Ice, and the latter would do the selling to dealers. For Jeremy and his friends, it was an easy solution—they didn't have to worry about collecting from their friends who were broke, could buy from their contacts in even greater quantities knowing they would never have any problems getting rid of the stuff, and now they could make real money.

The blue house at the end of the cul-de-sac was Jeremy's next destination. This time though he wasn't delivering Ice's goods, but rather his own. Drugs, drugs, and more drugs. All courtesy of Ice's contacts. He skirted around the side of the house carrying the large box. It was by far the largest drop Jeremy ever had to make and he had to cab it; no way he could carry it perched on the handlebars of his bike. He was pretty good at doing that, balancing boxes on them but this was too large and heavy—he needed both arms to carry it.

The drugs had been already paid for by Ice and all Jeremy had to do was leave the box around the back, in a crawl space. The opening was obscured by some upright boards. "All this cloak and dagger stuff," Jeremy said disdainfully. He would have preferred to deliver it directly to the Esperantos' clubhouse but Ice told him that was not a good idea; this was his deal alone and he didn't need his biker friends in on it. The more bodies, the smaller your cut becomes, Ice told Jeremy. But the good thing was that with the finances out of the way, Jeremy didn't have to hang around. Just drop and dash.

There it was, in clear sight. He removed the boards and pushed open a swinging half-door. *Probably a place for the old milkmen to make deposits*, thought Jeremy. He had read about those archaic times, complete with glass milk bottles and cream.

"Stay where you are!"

That voice, Jeremy had heard it before but couldn't quite place it. Startled, he jerked his head around.

"Mohawk Boy, you've got some explaining to do," said Detective Jackson, stepping out of the shadows into plain view. He walked over to where the box was and cut the top open with a penknife.

"What have we got here?" he said rhetorically, holding up plastic bags of pure white cocaine.

"I don't know anything about that," protested Jeremy. "I'm just a delivery guy, that's all."

They were all out now, at least half a dozen men and women with shiny badges. Amidst the carnage of putrid law enforcement officers, Jeremy saw the old woman who has passed away on his steps. The newspaper woman.

"What the fuck!" said Jeremy.

"Just a little trick of the trade," said Jackson. "Willa here has played dead a number of times. Too bad you didn't check her breathing, you might have noticed. And with a little pancake makeup ..."

"Holy shit. This is like a sting or something. Like from CSI. But you're barking up the wrong tree, Jackson. Me and my buds smoke a little dope, but for our own enjoyment. You took the Mexican Gold, you asshole. All the drugs in the world we had."

Jackson held up a few bags of coke once more.

"Like I told you, I'm just delivering," Jeremy said. "Why don't you believe me, asshole?"

"I wouldn't go around calling a police officer *an asshole*. It's not a very good idea, my friend." There stood Ice, a black holster hanging loosely around his oversized hips.

Jeremy sagged. "You big, fat turncoat! Wait'll I tell the guys in the Esperantos. You're dead meat."

They handcuffed Jeremy and put him in an unmarked squad car.

"We'll get your friends later," Ice said.

Jeremy spat, splattering Ice square in the face.

"Shouldn't have done that, my friend." He reared back and struck Jeremy smack in the eye, the very one he had once coloured himself.

Jeremy closed his eyes and cursed Ice. He then stuck his head out the window and yelled:

"Since the first Earth Day on April 22, 1970, we've lost more than one billion acres of forest! And each day, 27,000 trees are cut down to make toilet paper! The two-ply and 3-ply ones! The wet wipes! The ones with little squares and triangles, flowers, pattern toilet paper! And it's these assholes in uniform that are responsible, they're always wiping their asses!"

Ice pushed Jeremy's head back inside. "Shut up, Mohawk Boy."

"Why don't you wipe yourself with leaves instead!"

With further encouragement from Ice, who punched him in his other eye, Jeremy settled down, fingering both swollen eyes. Then he started crying. It wasn't the pain that caused the tears to come, nor the fact that he was facing charges. No, it was for his lost life. And for the very first time that he could remember, a feeling of sadness swept over him.

He looked down at his t-shirt, which was red with blood. He wondered whether there was anyone on earth who was going through what he was. And he concluded that there was no one. Then, his eyes continuing to swell and slowly close, he lost the ability to see anything at all and everything went completely dark. Now he knew, the apocalypse had truly come.

Acknowledgements

Earlier versions of the following stories appeared previously:

"Sleepless" — *Horizon Magazine*
"Butterfly Dreams" — *The Nashwaak Review*
"The Doctor Is in" — *Fevered Spring Anthology*
"The Quantum Theory of Love and Madness — *Inscribed*
"The Writer" — *All Rights Reserved*
"Paris Was the Rage" — *The Flaneur*
"Dating at your Peril" — *Parchment*
"Earth Day" — *Inscribed*
"New Year's at the Laundromat" — in the short story
    collection *Urban Legend* (Thistledown Press)

I'm indebted to Guernica Editions for believing in these stories and to Michael Mirolla for his wisdom in helping to shape them.

About the Author

Originally from Montreal, Jerry Levy now resides in Toronto, and works f/t in the corporate world. With a lifelong love of literature, his short stories have appeared in many literary magazines throughout Canada, the U.S., and the U.K. He has served as a judge for the Writer's Union of Canada's annual Short Prose Contest for a number of years, reading 20 stories and advancing three to the next round. And he occasionally does a similar task for the humanitarian organization Ve'ahavta, judging short stories from people who are marginalized and who have experienced homelessness. In 2013, a collection of 14 stories—*Urban Legend*—was published by Thistledown Press.